ALSO BY

CHRISTELLE DABOS

HERE, AND ONLY HERE

CHRISTELLE DABOS

HERE
AND ONLY
HERE

Translated from the French
by Hildegarde Serle

Europa
editions

CHRISTELLE DABOS

HERE, AND ONLY HERE

Translated from the French
by Hildegarde Serle

Europa
editions

Europa Editions
27 Union Square West, Suite 302
New York NY 10003
www.europaeditions.com
info@europaeditions.com

Copyright © 2023 by Christelle Dabos
First published in French by Gallimard Jeunesse
First publication 2023 by Europa Editions

Translation by Hildegarde Serle
Original title: *Ici et seulement Ici*
Translation copyright © 2023 by Europa Editions

Library of Congress Cataloging in Publication Data is available
ISBN 978-1-60945-956-7

Dabos, Christelle
Here, and Only Here

Art direction by Emanuele Ragnisco
instagram.com/emanueleragnisco

Cover design by Ginevra Rapisardi

Prepress by Grafica Punto Print – Rome

Printed in the USA

Contents

Third Term

New School Year

HERE,
AND ONLY
HERE

First Term

Iris

She let my hand go. Didn't even wait until Mom's car had turned the corner. I look at what's left of her face under that mass of hair. She got trashy this summer. Bad make-up, hair-dye disaster. She didn't say why she let my hand go. No need to: I get it. I've been getting it for ages. I got Dad's illness. I got Mom remarrying. I got every pregnancy that followed. No one explains anything to me, but I get things the way a weathervane knows the way the wind's blowing. So, I get that it's over for hands. It's a law in the new world—which is much older than me—that's about to swallow me up on the other side of the gate.

You won't have a sis, Here.

Fine. I slow down and let her get ahead in the back-to-school scramble, walk through the gate when my turn comes. The buildings draw my gaze upwards. The sun makes the yellow walls even yellower and the green shutters even greener. There's a ginormous clockface, and it's not even showing the right time: 2:28 P.M. I brace myself. Under the paint, plaster, and cement, inside the walls, deep in the invisible, I detect something I can't yet name, something seriously fierce that inhabits the whole school and is seeping into my bones. That will soon be part of me.

There's nothing playful about this playground. It stinks of drains and tar. I hope that at least I don't smell. Recently, something bushy has sprouted from my armpits; I get rid

13

of it as soon as I can with the stepfather's razor. I search for any familiar faces in the crowd; I find some. Old classmates from elementary school who are clinging to the straps of their school bags. Do I also have the panicked look of a parachutist? Émile is there. We shared the same desk every year. I ate his beet, he ate my spinach. He spots me and smiles, relieved to have a cheek to slap a kiss on, at last. We held hands, often. We hold hands right now.

"Let's hope we're in the same class," he says to me.

I don't reply. I do what I do best: I stand in the right place, neither too far ahead, nor too far behind, and I observe. It's because I observe that I get it. I see what my old classmates, including Émile, haven't yet noticed. A gap is forming in the schoolyard, between us and all the others. Last year, we were *the big ones*; today, we're back to being *the little ones*. I observe. We're too tense, too neat, too extra, too obvious. And I get it. All that I learned in my first schoolyard, just a few streets from here and already so far away, I must swiftly erase from my mind.

My sister has found some friends on a bench. Even her laughter is trashy. Ingrid. We've got names that resemble each other, but as for me, no way do I want to resemble her.

A bell rings. We're rounded up under the shelter, us, the little newbies. The principal and the teachers blather on. Welcome speech, instructions to be followed. I listen to none of it. I'll have plenty of time to read the school rules somewhere or other. Here, now, I'm too busy figuring out the other rules, those that aren't written down, those that are unspoken, those that no one imposes but everyone obeys. Backpacks slung over just one shoulder. Sneakers worn without socks. Earrings to be silver. Scruffiness that's carefully contrived. And everywhere in the schoolyard, in the bodies,

in the corridors, that something I still can't, as yet, define.
Something both hostile and thrilling.

They take attendance, then we're dispatched. Our old
gang from elementary school blown apart.

I merge into the row, among other girls and boys my
age. I memorize the faces of my new class. Émile joins his.
Three steps separate us: an intercontinental fault. His fingers,
stranded, seem still to seek mine. His mouth quivers. His
nose runs onto his lip. My eyes, which I'm determined to
keep dry, avoid his, and I hear bursts of laughter from the
big ones.

You won't blubber, Here.

Fine. For Émile, too, it's over for hands.

Pierre

Oh great, you little sniveling brat, you don't waste any time, do you? Sniveling like that, in front of the whole school, on your first day Here? You'll go far, you sniveler, you'll go very far, maybe even to the toilets from hell, over there, behind the sports ground. That's what got me sniveling.

That and the odd number.

I shove my hands deep in my pockets, my chin down on my neck, my head between my shoulders. This doesn't make me particularly inconspicuous, but how to put it . . . it's habit. Even over the summer, in the stifling shade of my room, high on anti-mosquito spray, fanned air, and blaring rap, I slumped. Now I trudge up the stairs. In front of me, twenty-six backs are bursting out of sleeveless tees. Some arched, some muscular, some plump, some tattooed, some hunched—but not as hunched as me. Twenty-six backs that I stared at for my entire first year Here.

What if things were different, this time around?

Second floor. One higher than last year, one lower than next year. All floors are the same. Checkered floor tiles, epileptic neon lights, doors that slam, graffiti galore. There are even shoe prints on the ceiling. Not the sort from throwing sneakers up in the air, oh no, the traces of steps taken, left, right, left, right, from one end of the corridor to the other. It's Théophile, the upside-down student, who made them. I haven't seen Théophile, not yet—apparently, he hangs out on all the school's ceilings. Don't know if he really exists, but it wouldn't be the weirdest thing I've seen Here.

"Hurry up, hurry up."

Stressed out already, our teacher. He keeps pulling off and putting back the caps of worn-out marker pens that leave only phantom letters on the board. The day's date squeaks out onto it. Everyone settles in their place, unpacks their things, reclaims their territory: chewing gum stuck inside the drawer, initials carved with a utility knife. Two chairs per desk, of course, and, of course, I'm on my own at the back of class.

The odd number. The jack of spades. The lousy kid, even though I've never had lice, even though I'm neither fat, nor scrawny, nor greasy. Just the odd one over.

I sit down. For now, my desk's perfectly aligned with the others in my row, to within a pube's breadth. It had been just like that on my very first day, I remember, and yet I still ended the year stuck to the wall. It was down to the legs of the desk. They edged backwards little by little. I tried to fight it. I'd put my desk back in place when classes were over. Next morning, every time, it had edged right back again; yup, during the night. A game like that, just let it go, bit like the footprints on the ceiling, gotta accept the phenomenon, end of.

New year, new floor, new classroom, new desk. What if things were different, this time around?

Bell. Math. Bell. Social Studies. Bell. Literature. One teacher follows another, all exasperated by the markers that mark nothing. It's getting warmer and warmer; my bangs are sticking to my eyebrows. The windows don't let any air in. A scorcher. I stare at the backs. Chairs are tipping. I spot papers, cans, smokes, videos being swapped: the dealing's back on already. And the bullying. I'm hypervigilant. I'm expecting an eye suddenly to meet mine, that they'll all remember my existence, and the consequences that'll have.

Nothing. No one clocks me. My desk doesn't move. In the cafeteria, same thing, I pass unnoticed between the egg mayo and the expired yogurt. All around me, mayhem and menace, hollering and hugging. They're the sea, I'm the reef.

What if things were really different, this time around?

I spend the afternoon with my head turned to the window, watching the pigeons shit on the benches in the schoolyard. I'm clammy, the pen slips between my fingers. Don't know if it was lunch or what, but there's some serious grumbling in my bowels. Right. The ultimate test. We get a short recess between each lesson. The classrooms empty out and the bathrooms fill up, just to grab a few minutes away. Usually, I stay in class on my own, but right now, it's urgent.

I hug the walls of the entire corridor.

Stand outside the door to the bathroom.

Walk in.

The laughter stops. Through the cigarette smoke, all faces suddenly turn to me. That's it. For the first time since walking through the gate this morning, they see me. Not a word between them, not a word to me. They punch straight and they punch hard. I'm pushed around, and gobbed on, and shoved back over the boundary I'd crossed. And I know, while spitting out the TP they stuffed in my mouth and charging down the stairs, suddenly seeing horribly clearly, my gut killing me, yes, I know that from tonight onwards, my desk will start edging back again; from tomorrow onwards, all the harrying will resume.

I cross the schoolyard, skirt the sports ground, enter the

toilets from hell: sickening stench, permanently blocked pipes. I hit the familiar seat, the only one I've been allowed to squat on since arriving Here. Empty my bowels. It's no good lingering in the toilets from hell—the longer you stay, the more you want to stay, and I'm already feeling the effects, maybe of the walls, maybe of the smells, but rather, I think, of what makes tables move backwards and ceilings be walked over, something embedded in every crevice of the school, shrinking me from all directions, and the lighter I become, the more I slump, every muscle in my back relaxes, I'm humiliated and happy as never before. I sob with relief.

No, things won't be different this time around.

I'm the odd number, the jack of spades, the lousy kid, and no one can take that away from me.

Madeleine

Horses.

Louise was forever drawing them. In profile, three-quarter view, and full-face, yes, even full-face. Whenever I drew a horse full-face, the teacher thought it was a bottle. Louise's horses? Works of art. Realer than real. She'd play with shading to add contours, create hollows, make manes, nostrils, muscles, bone structure leap out from the paper . . . And the eyes, powerfully dark, with just enough brightness between the lashes. What depth in the eyes of Louise's horses! I got the lovely feeling, when poring over her sketches, of plunging to the very bottom of a well.

Phalluses.

That's what Louise is drawing today, in the margin of her page, with a 2B pencil. I hate the 2B. It's oily and it makes a yukky noise. I only have HBs in my pencil case, only rose windows in my notebook. I gave up full-face horses for paper stained-glass windows. I draw them with a compass and then color them in, pressing hard on the lead for the outlines, then gently between each line, with light, oblique strokes that must never, ever go over the line. If they do go over, or my hand accidentally smudges the coloring, I rip up the page and pinch my thigh.

Louise's 2B is scrawling some obscenity on the rose window I've just finished. Her faint smile is swiftly dropped. The light from the projector makes her appear even bleaker to me. The teacher's showing us slides from museums she visited on her travels. Art. At elementary school, it was our fave subject. Or rather, the subject we most liked to compare ourselves at. Now, Louise doesn't compare herself with me anymore. Doesn't need to anymore. She's bored. She was already bored last year, and the year before that. She's bored Here. Despite me. Because of me. A whole summer without seeing each other, without phoning each other, and we're already struggling to find a subject of conversation. She talks to me about films I haven't seen, I talk to her about books she hasn't read. It wasn't so complicated between us at the time of the horses. If we ever were friends, we've forgotten how to do it, but we stay together, despite the silences, because it protects us from the class. Hanging around alone, Here, is like becoming an odd one over, and that does scare me. It scares Louise, too, I think.

"I saw one this summer."

Louise barely lowers her voice. The slides roll on. Searing flashes in the darkness. I shake my head; I don't understand. With her 2B, she draws another phallus. Her eyes glint in the neat frame of her square bob. Silky hair. Silky voice. Silky skin. Fourteen years old, just like me. She looks eleven. She's kept a supple, soft body, flat as a board, deceptively intact, whereas puberty is running riot over mine. She looks at me with a look that's not really looking.

"It's like swallowing seawater."

Her lips half-open. Shadows and brightness, like the eyes of her old horses. Here we go. I'd like to put my fingers in my ears, not listen to her, not let her taint me, not already, not on the very first day, not the new me, the person I became on 31 August. I pinch my thigh.

"And you, d'you meet anyone during your vacation?"

There's something judgmental in her question.

Condemning. Disappointed in advance. No, Louise doesn't compare herself with me anymore. She knows me well enough to know that I had no genital encounters, close or distant. No contact, ever, with anyone, or even between me and me. In the shower, I use the spray from the hand-held head; in the bathroom, three layers of toilet paper.

"No."

It's a lie, which I pay for with another pinch of my thigh, but, in all conscience, am at ease with. Louise leans back on her chair, voluptuously, though I don't like that word. I know a whole load of words, but few find favor with me. Speaking spoils everything. It's like telling a dream, and my dreams, they can't be told. The one of 31 August, less so than the rest—I even scratched the date, with the point of my compass, onto the wallpaper in my bedroom, between the wardrobe and the bookcase. A secret pact. And yet, I was starting to despair. Books that were less and less satisfying, a life that was more and more faked. In the torpor of a siesta, I sought a way out, far away from the ugliness, beyond this bulky body that weighs me down more every day, and that sweats and oozes and bleeds.

And that's when it happened.

A dazzling light beneath my eyelids. A voice in my left ear, an awesome voice. It said to me: "You Are Chosen" (yes, yes, I heard the capital letters). When I woke up, my muscles were taut, my calves rock-hard, and my left ear was ringing, painfully. I instantly knew that nothing would ever be as before, that I was being steered to embrace a destiny that was out of the ordinary, that the revolution in my world, in the whole world, was imminent.

And since that dream of 31 August, everything has been exactly the same as before.

Pimples have continued to erupt on my chin, the TV news hasn't announced a single apocalypse, and the first day of term did, in the end, arrive. I've looked out for the signs. I looked out for them as I went through the gate this morning. I looked out for them during every hour in class, and every recess. I'm looking out for them right now, in the classroom, between two flashes of slide and two pinches of thigh. Because I've been Chosen, with the capital letter, I don't know by whom, or why, but everything is just about to change; thanks to me; me with whom Louise has stopped comparing herself; me who'll now no longer need to compare myself with her.

End of the slideshow. The teacher claps her hands to wake us up.

"A volunteer to reopen the shutters."

I jump up before Louise, every teacher's pet, thinks of doing so. It's me this school needs. I wrestle with the rusty catches of the window. In a few seconds the bell will go, lessons over. Something's going to happen. Something has to happen.

Here.

I push open the green shutters. A shadow shoots out of the sun, skims over my head, swirls across the room, draws cries from the whole class, yes, even Louise, swoops over the desks, then leaves through the window just as it had arrived.

The bell shrieks. The teacher sighs:

"Right. A volunteer to clean up that pigeon's droppings."

I gaze at the white feather that has fallen at my feet. I smile. There we are. That's the signal. My new life is finally going to begin.

Guy

What the hell's that name, there, under mine? The list is written in chalk on the old blackboard . . . what's that expression again? *Like in the olden days.* When I started at this school, at the beginning of the very beginning, the blackboard was already on the first floor. And when we entered the second year, me and the rest of the class, the board moved up to the second floor with us. Ditto for the third year. And double ditto today: here it is, on the wall of the fourth floor, the very top floor, up the most stairs, which I've just had to climb, seeing as the elevator, hey, it's for the teachers and the principal (and the prince). Don't even know who unscrews this board for us, lugs it up for us, and re-screws it for us each time. It's always there, faithful as ever, in its new position, on the Monday we all get back.

And from the Tuesday, as usual, the list's on it. Except that this year, the name under mine, right there, I've no idea who that is.

"Oh, right, so we've got our pairs?"

It's Ariane who's turned up. She looks like she fell out of bed. Out of the bus, too. She's clearly not a morning person. Her heels make a crazy racket in the corridor. Normally, it's against the rules, heels like that, but Ariane's never been hit with a single warning. Same here, not one, when I do fuck all in class. But then, hey, that's normal: on the list, we're both among the Tops.

24

All the same, what the hell's that name, there, under mine?

Ariane manages a fake kiss that doesn't really touch my cheek, a less than half-hearted one, which at first warms me, then chills me. Ariane was my first crush and my first blow-off. She's brought her supermarket basket, and I've got mine. It's obvious she's not that thrilled to be on collection duty with me, but hey, orders are orders.

"I'm cursed."

Ariane has just read the blackboard. She covers her face with her hands, but not for long because it's unworthy of a Top. The name under hers . . . oh yeah, that one I do know. I let out a laugh that even I think sounds pathetic.

"You've got the lousy girl?"

"I'm beyond cursed."

It's one of the things I don't really get, Here. That way everyone has of switching into "malediction" mode, as if it was really true. Personally, I don't believe in either good luck, or bad luck. Well, I believe I don't believe in them.

"But that's not possible," I go to Ariane. "She's an odd one over. She can't be paired up. Not even as a Bottom."

"This year she can."

"Why's that?"

"Because of the foreign girl, dickhead. It changes the order. We're not the same number in class, the balance is thrown. The lousy girl stops being a lousy girl, and it's me who's stuck with her all year."

So, we've got a foreign girl? Is that her name, there, under mine? I didn't clock her at all yesterday; that'll teach me for sleeping on the desk, but hey ho, I try to tell myself that she can't be worse than the lousy girl or Christophe. He was my pair last year, Christophe, and I seriously didn't think it possible to be more useless than me at grammar and comp.

I got a shitload of zeros on my work and a right walloping at home. The list only works at school. To my parents, I'm not a Top. I'm a great fat nothing.

"Ask the prince," I go to Ariane.

"Ask him what?"

"To put you with another Bottom girl. Or Bottom guy. You might be able to swap."

The look Ariane throws at me. She barely reaches my chin, now, despite her starlet heels, and yet I still feel small.

"Seriously, dickhead, you still don't get it? It's not the prince who writes the list."

"Who is it then?"

Ariane is . . . what's that word again? *Dismayed*, that's it. I often have that effect.

"How on earth can you, of all people, be a Top? It's beyond me."

I laugh, even though inside I don't really feel like it. It's beyond everyone. The list isn't about who's popular with the girls, or who's got the biggest one among the boys. I can't really remember when it first started. One winter? One spring? In any case, it was in our first year. The names of everyone in our class written in chalk, two by two, one name on top, then a line, one name on the bottom, like fractions but with letters instead of numbers. Our class was cut in two, easy as a pear, that day. The pairs change every year, but one thing has never changed: the Tops have always stayed Tops, and the Bottoms always stayed Bottoms. It's only our class that has such a list. And it's only our class that has such a prince. I always thought it was down to him, the stunt of the names on the board, especially as his name's never on it.

If it's not him, then who is it? Who's paired me up with the foreign girl?

The bell will go off soon, we mustn't forget the collection. The others are starting to turn up and file past the board. The Tops, the Bottoms. Everyone wants to know who they've been paired with for the year. There's some who smile, some who pull a face. But the list is the list. Me and Ariane, we stand around at the front of the class with our baskets. We let the Tops come in. Ariane gives them each a kiss, the real thing, making a sound at once dry and moist that resonates weirdly in my belly. I try to shake hands with some almost-bros.

The prince arrives. He doesn't respond to my "hi," but hey, he doesn't respond to those of the others, either. Everyone avoids looking directly at him; it's forbidden. He sits on his usual chair. In the middle of the classroom. Alone. No pair for the prince.

Then it's the Bottoms' turn. Me and Arianne hold out the baskets. We collect cash and smokes (lights don't count, weed counts double.) I scope all the Bottoms. I'm looking for the foreign girl; I don't find her. I don't let on in front of the others, but it's creeping me out, this girl I don't know and who doesn't know me, either. On top of that, I've never been paired with one—a girl—myself. It's not that I'm already fantasizing or anything; I don't even consider Bottom girls, on principle. But I did try my luck with all the Top girls in my class. Not one of them said yes. Losing face, that's the worst that can happen. So I keep my head down, make out it's me who's no longer interested, and too bad that it's shameful, quitting school at the end of the year without having made out, it's still less shameful than only ever getting blown off.

The collection's nearly finished. Ariane's basket is full; she's better at it than me. The lousy girl—sorry, the ex-lousy girl—almost sobbed with joy at seeing her name under

27

Ariane's on the board, but she didn't, phew, because blubbing in front of everyone, forget it, it's a punishable offence;
anyhow, she didn't blub but she did pay her share for the
very first time, even paid more than expected, while saying
thanks-thanks-thanks to Ariane, who refrained from slap-
ping her, seeing as now, hey, she's paid and you don't slap
those who pay, unless they blub, that's the rule. I feel a bit
uneasy all the same.

Meanwhile, still no foreign girl to be seen. I've got Christophe trying to negotiate with me. He didn't cough up a
quarter of what he owes us into the basket. Yet he knows
how it works. He pays: he gets peace until the following
month's collection. He doesn't pay: we make life miserable
for him until he does pay.

"Come on, dude," he goes to me. "Chill. I've no cash on
me right now. I'll make up for it tomorrow, without fail,
with interest."

I'd already gotten this whole cash-strapped number when
he was my Bottom. A bad payer, that Christophe, as well
as being bad at everything else. I swipe his high-tops and
stuff them in the basket. They're no big brand, but not trash
either. With a bit of luck, they'll be the prince's size. The
teacher might arrive late on purpose so as not to witness
our little affairs, but he won't be long now. Everyone in class
is sitting in their new place, pair by pair, Top with Bottom,
Ariane with the ex-lousy girl, and the prince bang in the
middle. Everyone except me, still stuck at the door, kicking
my heels. I can feel a fuck of a panic rising. What if she never
turned up, this foreign girl? What if that made me an odd
one over? The new lousy kid?

And just then, I spot her: a student never seen before. In
the corridor, in front of the list, chalk in hand, she's writing.

She's writing on the board. A total no-no. I pounce on her and snatch away her chalk.

"You can't do that. You must never do that."

Eyebrows. I could almost forget the rest, but I stalled on her eyebrows, maybe because they form just one brow, linked by a little bridge of hairs above the nose. On the board, the harm's done: a thick chalk line, just like the brow, right between my name and hers. The foreign girl has added a line *above* the line, and I twig that it's no longer a dividing line at all.

It's an "equals" sign.

29

Iris

"Get a move on, Émile."

I look at myself. It's not me in the mirror of the restroom. In fact, it could be any girl in my class. Same rings, same curls, same barrettes, same straps, same bracelets, same jewelry, same blusher, same blouse, and, of course, same store. All my allowance has gone to that store. I asked the stepfather for money, pinched some from my sister's coin purse, and busted my elementary-school bag so Mom would buy me one with no shame attached, which I sling over just one shoulder, and so fucking what if that does my back in.

The price of fitting in.

"Émile, get a move on."

The sound of flushing. Émile finally emerges. He fumbles with his belt, trying to act normal, but it's impossible not to notice that his mug is all puffy.

"Pee through your eyes now, do you?"

I'm teasing him, but he's not amused. Émile was never as pitiful as this before. Or maybe I didn't look at him the same way. He soaps his hands at the sink, runs the faucet for a long time, dawdles on purpose. He's in no hurry to return to recess; I am. Being conspicuous by your absence, it's as good a way as any to get noticed. I look at his skinny arms, poking out of his T-shirt sleeves like popsicle sticks, and then I look at the girl in the mirror, a shadow against the light from the corridor, this me who isn't me. A me who isn't Ingrid, either, and that's what matters most: this year, my sister's decided to make all her clothes herself. Yes. Herself. As if she didn't stick out enough already.

"I'm not going to be lookout in the girls' restroom all year."

Émile freezes, hands full of suds; hands that I've never again touched. His shoulder blades tremble under the T-shirt.

"They don't let me . . . into the bathroom. It's only with you that I can . . ."

I know. I knew it from the very first pee break. The bathrooms, Here, are places of power. I've seen so many negotiations in the first-floor bathrooms alone: math homework traded for reading tests, crib-sheet swaps, wheeling and dealing, every kind of forfeit and "dare you!", even so far as sneakily stuffing your undies into a teacher's bag. And voting, every day more voting, with the toilet cubicles as polling booths, to decide with a majority vote who's the most stylish, the nicest, the most amazing, and I brace myself at every vote count, hoping my name won't appear on any paper, be it positive or negative. Makes you wonder what goes on in the bathrooms on the floors above, where the older kids are.

"Could we eat together, in the cafeteria?"

Émile doesn't ask, he implores. I think of the spinach he'd eat for me, and the beet I'd eat for him, and then quit thinking about it.

"We can't. We're not in the same class."

"But we're still in the same schoolyard. It does count, the schoolyard. D'you remember how we'd play in our old one?"

Yup, I do occasionally have the very haziest visions of skipping elastics, sponge balls, badly drawn hopscotch grids, bouncing marbles . . . remnants of an ancient domain where everything that shone in the light—sequins, stones, beads, plums, parquets, plastic—was extraordinary. But no, truly, I find it hard to imagine that that was my life. A few days Here and, poof—amnesia.

"There's no playing in that one," I reply.

Seems like Émile hasn't quite finished flushing himself out: his eyes threaten to well up again. He stinks of fear. At middle school, the worst isn't the lessons, it's all that happens in between them. The very consistency of time is different Here. Recesses are eternities. It's not that they're boring, oh no, boredom at least has something mellow, almost comfortable about it. No, we spend every second of every minute fighting the fear of putting a foot wrong, while pretending to have fun.

For Émile, it's already too late. And I can't help but relent: "We'll see."

I look down the corridor I'm supposed to keep watch on. They're heading this way: nearly all the girls in my class. No time to warn Émile. They walk in and their rings, their curls, their barrettes, the whole flashy lot comes to an abrupt stop. A boy, in *their* place, that boy no less, it's more than a territorial invasion, it's an infestation. The girls look at Émile, and then at me, and then at Émile again. His hands are dripping with lather.

"Pervert."

No voting. The verdict is instantaneous. Unanimous. My knees are knocking. I've heard about the fate reserved for perverts Here. It's worse than for odd ones.

Émile panics.

"I just used the bathroom, that's all! Tell them I just used the bathroom!"

The girls look back at me. All of them. Too many eyes. I say nothing.

"Close the door," they say.

I close the door. I close my eyes, too. I'd said, "We'll see" to Émile. Too late for seeing now.

The Top-Secret Club

Number One: "Right. First, thanks for being here, all of you, the faithful to the cause. Last year wasn't easy. Many failures. Many losses, too. Before beginning this first meeting of the new term, let's all, if you'd care to, spare a thought for our dearly departed ones. Pilou and Cookie, who died while doing their duty, and because Number Six forgot to punch some holes in their box. Bip-Bip, struck down by a heart attack in the twilight of his life, and that's after as good as beating the record for wheel revolutions per minute. And even within the ranks of the humans, yes, even among us, the losses have been heavy. We're thinking of you, Number Three, sent to that faraway hospital from which you've never returned.

Number Three: "Yes, yes I have. I have returned. I never even left."

Number One: "A heavy toll, then, but not entirely futile. Because if we did experience failures, we also made some solid progress. Number Two, please, read us the expert's end-of-year report."

Number Two: "I'm just looking for it, fuck's sake . . . I put it in my natural-science folder. Anyone seen my nat-sci file? I put it down right there and it's disappeared. As if by chance, when the report happened to be inside it. *It* knows, fuck's sake! *It* knows and *it* doesn't want us to know. First the folder, and then what? *It's* going to make us disappear one after the other! We're in the process of touching on things that shouldn't be . . . oh, my mistake, the folder was still in my bag. Here's the expert's report. Shall I read it, then?"

Number One: "Please."

Number Two: "'A year and four months after founding the Top-Secret Club, conset . . . consic . . . consecutive to several series of experiments, each following a protocol of extreme scientific rigor and based on reliable auditory and oclu . . . ocular evidence'—fuck's sake, when does this sentence end?—'we can today confirm with certainty the presence of a phenomenon that we have called the *intramural distortion of the field of reality*, a phenomenon observed from the main gate to, and including, the toilets from hell. We are able to provide, in order to dismiss all skepi . . . sketi . . . skepticism, at least one positive proof of the aforementioned phenomenon cited above.' Fuck's sake, do I have to read to the end? We already know all this."

Number One: "It's indispensable. Repetition is the mother of science."

Number Two: "Okay, okay. 'Our proof of the *intramural distortion of the field of reality* is an unidentified substance that we have called "the schmoil." The schmoil is the very reason the Top-Secret Club was founded, when Number One discovered its existence forti . . . fortuitously in one of the school's gutters, used to drain away dirty water. One aspect sepci . . . spefic . . . specific to the schmoil is that it runs in the gutter just once a week, always on a Thursday and always very precisely at 2:28 P.M., but *never during the school holidays*.' (That bit's written slanty.) 'This conclusion has been established based on the viewing of hundreds of hours of videos since recorded by the camera belonging to the grandfather of Number Six.'"

Number Six: "He's an old fool. Never even knew how to use it. Didn't even notice it wasn't in the drawer anymore."

Number Two: "Shut up. 'We were unable to establish the provenance of the schmoil. It was for the sake of scientific truth that we ourselves tested its pop . . . properties. The schmoil is of a liquid consistency, barely thicker than water. The schmoil is of a color that we unanimously qualified as "cow's milk."' Fuck's sake, what is it now?"

Number Five: "Can I go for a pee while you carry on?"

Number Two: "No. If I'm reading, you listen. Where was I? 'The schmoil is totally odorless. The schmoil is not edible, if we go by the unprecedented gastric consequences it caused among the volunteers who ingested it. The schmoil is not corrosive, either, but did prove to be highly inflammable when in contact with a reagent from the chemistry set of the late-lamented Number Three.'"

Number Three: "No, c'mon, just quit the stupid-ass whining."

Number Two: "'The most notable property of the schmoil is the alteration of mood it causes in subjects in its immediate vicinity. Among creatures such as insects, mice, hamsters, and lizards, we have observed a very sudden hypra . . . hyperactivity. Among humans, outbursts of hilarity, irac . . . irsac . . . irascibility, nay . . .' aha, you've written ney with an a, mistake! ' . . . nay aggression. The effects of the schmoil fade after about twenty minutes. They are non-existent an hour after it has been flushed from the drains. We currently have at our disposal nineteen samples in test tubes stored in a secure place.' There, I'm done."

Number One: "Thanks, Number Two. So, has that refreshed everyone's memory? Do you now all remember why we gather every day? The discovery of the schmoil, and thereby of the irrefutable proof of the existence of the *intra-mural distortion of the field of reality*, has vested us with a crucial mission. We have the moral duty to look for additional proof. We have the responsibility to record, study, interpret each incident reported to us, or that we witness ourselves, those things that only occur within this establishment, and that, once back home with our parents, in our bedrooms, in the evening, seem absurd to us, nay (with an 'a', actually, Number Two) unreasonable. I've considered it all summer and I think I can confirm to you, without error, to you, the faithful to the cause, that it's that, and only that, that will bring us the solution."

Number Four: "The solution to what?"

Number One: "To the end of the world, of course. The one that will occur on a Thursday, at 2:28 P.M. Here."

Pierre

I've got a schnozbleed. These things happen when you get a ball straight in the mug for the seventh time. The trick is not to move, not to flinch, just take it. Too often I've seen, in other classes' sports lessons, odd ones who try to protect their faces, or, the pits, go off to hide in the changing-room. As for me, I sit tight in my proper place, on the touchline bench, where my whole class expects me to be. I watch them play, those twenty-six classmates, thirteen against thirteen, not that sure what game they're playing in fact, and probably they aren't either—even the teacher has given up refereeing and is having a smoke somewhere between the gym and the tennis court. They knock the ball around with their feet, grip it with their hands, occasionally shoot it into the goal, more often into the wilderness, and I'm up double-quick to go fetch it. When a side loses—think they've lost, at any rate, seeing as the rules aren't clearly defined—there's always one to come and vent his frustration on me. My T-shirt is drenched in gobs of spit. Especially those of Jérémie; got competition running in his veins, has Jérémie. Saliva specially hawked up for me.

I'm happy.

The sports lesson is really the only time in the week when I see something other than the backs of my classmates. From my bench, I notice all those small details that escape me the rest of the time: new glasses, braces, grazed knees, budding boobs, moles, acne scars. They're not exactly top models, my classmates, but what really matters is that I need them as much as they need me. After all, what stops them from whacking each other's nut when fighting over the ball, is knowing they can help themselves to mine.

Sniff.

I suddenly get a nasty whiff. At first, I think it's the blood dripping from my nose, but that smell, no, it's coming from somewhere else, from a distance, somewhere dark and dense. It stinks as much as the toilets from hell, over there, behind the sports grounds, and the stench without the walls, well, dunno, gives me the creeps.

I hunch over even more. Something's trying to become denser, there, now, close by. But what?

On the pitch, no one but me seems to smell the funk. But they're all hollering at each other, opponents, teammates, boys, girls. There isn't even a ball in play anymore. Total mayhem. Jérémie's threatening to bury his fist in someone's face. I don't get how it's gone to pot so fast. My role, my raison d'être is to avoid exactly what's now happening.

And then, I see it.

In the middle of the pitch, between all the stamping sneakers, where I swear, on my mother's life, I swear there was absolutely nothing: a bottle. A glass one. Empty. Offered up. Didn't take two seconds for someone to grab it and smash it on Jérémie's head.

Stunned silence.

Well, silence from the others. Because from Jérémie, it's more than a scream. He's curled up on the tarmac. His eyes have disappeared behind his hands, behind his howl, behind the blood, fuck, so much blood, red and black, the blood. The class stands frozen around him. Eyes dart. There's less interest in helping the victim than in finding the culprit. And the bottle, gone. The bottle, forgotten. Whereas me, all of a sudden, I'm remembered. I'm entitled to everyone's attention.

My raison d'être. I leap from the bench and break into a sprint. I charge towards the teacher, who, cig in mouth, is on her way back.

"Who's that bawling? What happened?"

No need to think. I reply:

"It's Jérémie, Miss. I smashed his head in."

I'm the odd number, the jack of spades, the lousy kid, and no one can take that away from me.

Guy

"An eye lost. Barely thirteen, the kid, and not leaving the hospital any time soon. Is that what they're teaching you, your teachers? To poke each other's eyes out? Enough to end up in the clink, a thing like that. Do you actually realize that it could've happened in your class? That it could've been you?"

"Me what? In the hospital or the clink?"

Uh-oh, my dad's face turns mean in the rearview mirror.

"What are we going to do with you."

Seems like a question, but isn't one at all. I pick at the peeling corner of the label of fares on the back window. It's pissing it down, outside.

"Just bringing home, to your mother and I, a decent grade, just one, wouldn't do us any harm. I'm not telling you to be gifted, I'm just asking you to tip the scales. To have some direction. Don't you have some homework to give in today?"

I glare at the traffic lights through the rain. Green, green, green, go on, green. To avoid the rearview mirror. A taxi driver: well, my dad sure knows where he's going. He has some *direction*. On day duty or night duty, makes no difference, he's sure to drop me off, on the dot, every morning at the gate, although, if I wasn't a fourth-floor Top, I'd have paid for it in punches. At my age, you go by bus, by scooter, by tram, on foot, on your hands, but you don't get a lift from Daddy.

Outside, the pavement. On the pavement, a raincoat. Under the hood, a brow.

"I'm getting out here."

Dad's livid when I slam his car door. I've never cut school before, but he doesn't give a shit, wants to see me walk through the gate. Seriously, where would I go?

I splash through all the puddles on the pavement.

"Hey!" I call out.

The foreign girl lifts her hood in my direction. I get the same shock as every time. It's not so much the brow as the eyes under it. No Bottom gives a look like that. No Top, either. It's as if those eyes didn't sleep, ever.

"My old man's spying on me. Wait till we're inside."

She says nothing. In fact, since she first arrived at school, she hasn't said much. That's normal, I suppose, for foreigners who just turn up here from wherever, they're bound to have to go through . . . what's that word, again? *Quarantine*. No close contact from us until we know what kind of dude we're dealing with. That one, that foreigner, I soon figured her out, seeing as we're side by side in class, but she's not easy to pin down. For a start, she doesn't eat in the cafeteria with us. She never comes to sports classes. She's an "unsupervised student," as written in her grade book. Soon as we get any free time, snap, she packs up her stuff and disappears. In class, she scribbles tons of notes. It's not enough for her to copy down what the teachers write on the board, oh no, she fills up the margins with comments that I, sitting close by, can't make out. At first, I thought I'd landed a star student, the kind who'd improve my grades and get on my wick, but then, when a teacher asks a question, she doesn't come up with the goods. Though sometimes, she's the one asking a question that even the teacher can't answer, and even the prince turns around in his chair, and everyone has to look down, because looking directly at the prince is forbidden. Whenever this happens, she screws up her eyes, there, under that brow that's like a flying bird, and turns them away, and seems to look deep, very deep within.

Anyway.

The foreign girl doesn't say much, but she does listen. And she listened very carefully, yesterday, when I looked her in the eye, and the eyebrow, before home time, and explained the ground rules to her: "You're my pair. You're a Bottom. You do my homework."

So today, I wait until we're under the shelter out of the rain where Dad's rearview mirror can't spy on me anymore, and I unzip my bag.

"Put the math worksheet in quick before a teacher shows up."

The foreign girl puts nothing in at all. But she does swipe my journal, and, calm as you like, flicks through it.

"What d'you think you're doing?"

"Getting acquainted."

"Acquainted with what? I haven't written a jot in it."

"Exactly."

Is she fucking around with me, this foreign girl? She doesn't seem to be. There's something super serious about her way of not reading what I've not written. The journal was bought for me by my mother, and she didn't scrimp—it's like a real fancy book, with leather binding and gilt edges, if you please, so as to make me feel totally . . . what's that word again? *Mortified.*

"Right, quick, the bell's gonna go. Hand over that worksheet."

The foreign girl puts the journal back in my bag. She looks

at me, head held high. Straight in the eye. Water is dripping off her hoodie onto her chin, we're getting buffeted from all directions under the shelter, where it stinks of damp raincoat, but I barely notice any of that. The foreign girl's eyes, they almost never blink.

"No thanks."

"You didn't get what I said yesterday?"

"I understood you very clearly. Here, there are rules. Your board, your list, your pairs, your Tops, your Bottoms, those are the rules. I've known other Heres which had their own rules. That's how it works, how it's always worked, everywhere. I respect that. But no thanks."

I zip up my bag.

"Don't take it personally, but I'm going to have to hit you."

"I know. It's part of the rules. Hit me. But I'll hit you, too."

I don't know what staggers me most. What she comes out with, or the way she comes out with it. Quick as a flash, but far too calmly. And I believe her. It's like it's written in chalk on her body. She's not at all hefty, she doesn't hold herself straight, but she's got something seriously solid about her. I know that if I give her a slap, she'll give me one right back. And I'm already not that keen on dishing out blows as it is, so receiving them . . .

The bell goes.

In four floors' time, if I don't have my math homework, I'll bag my first zero of the year and then face fury in mega close-up in Dad's rearview mirror. Worse. If in four floors' time I don't have my math homework, my reputation as a Top will take a knock and the prince will summon me to the toilets.

Never lose face.

"So what do we do?"

I ask that, but don't really expect an answer. And yet she, the foreign girl, does give me one, and that answer I was expecting even less:

"I help you to do your homework yourself."

Madeleine

"I want a scooter."

That's what Louise's fountain pen tattoos on my hand. The ink glistens for a few seconds before drying. I envy the neatness of the handwriting. Even though Louise doesn't draw anything beautiful anymore, everything that comes from her remains touched with grace.

And yet it's not her who's been Chosen.

I cross my arms on the desk and bury myself in them, head first. Rain on the windows, scraping of chairs, giggling, spitting contests, the smell of glue and spliffs: the study room encroaches on me from all directions. I disown it, just as I disown the heaviness of my flesh, the thickness of my skin, the bulkiness of my bones, and this grease that, day after day, takes over my hair. I open my eyes wide in the muggy murkiness of my arms. Taped inside my notebook, almost sticking to my lashes, the feather is there. I immerse myself in all that it represents. Closing my eyes isn't allowed, and too bad if they sting. I stare so hard at the feather, I become dazzled. So white in the dark! It promises me. *Soon.*

Louise digs me in the ribs with her elbow:

"You're as musty as your pigeon."

I close the notebook. It wasn't a pigeon, but that Louise didn't see. No one saw what I myself saw. No one's worthy of that. I pinch my thigh. Beware of the temptation to hate.

I sweep an eraser pen over my hand and rub on the words until all the ink's faded.

"Why a scooter?" I ask.

"To go somewhere else."

Far from Here, I understand. Except that it's Here that it's going to happen: what I've been Chosen for. I wait, day after day, to discover what it is. I gaze around the study room, where our free periods are spent. Three times bigger than our classroom, always full of people, never a supervisor. Dancing across the ceiling, miraculously, are the shoe prints, the same ones as on the second floor of the school. I've heard some rumors about Théophile, the upside-down student. A new boy escaping from hazing. A high-jump champion. An odd one so rejected by his class that he could no longer put a foot on the ground. Whatever the story, everyone agrees that Théophile has haunted the ceilings for years, and that he only shows himself to those he deems worthy.

Am I not worthy, I who have been Chosen? When's my awesome event going to happen?

"Oyez, young ladies!"

I look down from the ceiling. It isn't Théophile. It's just Ben. Same class, but the size of a sophomore, the look of a barman. He's the only student in the whole school who can get away with wearing a tie and a side parting without getting beaten up for it. He brings with him a light scent of rain, despite his dry shoes.

"Are you inclined to listen to the latest news bulletin?"

He addresses us in the plural, but the look he gives Louise is in the singular. A filthy look. He'd like her to pull on his tie and spoil him. I know that because I heard him saying it to the others. *To spoil*. A synonym of to rot.

Louise sighs. She's bored. The best grades in the class,

Louise, first in every subject, Louise, without ever opening a book or listening to a teacher. Born excellent.

"What is it, your news?"

"Today's weather forecast: showers."

"Anything else?"

"The prince on the fourth floor has issued a new decree."

"Does it concern us?"

"It concerns everyone. Looking directly at him is forbidden."

"Wasn't that already forbidden last year?"

"Well, it's re-forbidden this year."

"Why?"

"We don't know. It's re-forbidden, and that's it."

"Anything else?"

"The Top-Secret Club has resumed its meetings."

"Anything else?"

"A second-year student has been hospitalized. An odd one smashed a bottle in his eye, or something like that."

"Anything else?"

"There's a pervert in the first year."

Louise's lips quiver; almost a smile.

"Have you got a scooter, then, Ben?"

"Even better."

Ben unbuttons his smart jacket and opens it with a parody of discretion. Poking out of an inside pocket there's a candy tin. I've heard all about them, Ben's candies. They say everything seems dull after tasting them. An easy paradise, sure, but a paradise all the same.

He places one on the tip of his tongue. He smiles. He waits. Louise peels herself off her chair and sucks up the candy. She didn't hesitate a second over mixing her saliva with his. I pinch my thigh. The temptation to hate. Louise crunches the candy between her teeth; her eyes roll, wander far, far away.

"I want another one."

"Another time, perhaps. If you're nice."

Ben turns from Louise and ogles the excess that's me, which I hide as best I can under my baggiest sweaters.

He places another candy on his tongue. Smiles. Waits.

I think of the feather, of the dream of 31 August, of the voice in my left ear, and I feel myself sinking. Around us, all the gross childishness of the study room is endlessly replicated; my body remains seated, elbows on desk, legs under chair, but despite not moving, I'm going down. They're taking me down, all of them. What they do. What they aren't. Where's the way out? How can I save myself? How be saved? And what if, from the start, it was already too late? If it really was just a pigeon?

I rise. Something rises through me. Something scrutinizes Ben through me. And through me, something speaks; a powerful murmur. Capitalized.

"Touch Her And You Will Touch The Void. Within Everything There Exists A Vastness Darker Than The Most Impenetrable Of Darknesses. Touch Her And You Will Fall Into The Abyss Where Offenses Bear Down, Where Morals Break Down, And You Will Drag Your Mother Down With You, And You Will Drag Your Father Down With You. Touch Her, Benjamin: Never Again Will You Know Either The Gentle Or The Mild."

I fall silent. It's over, but it continues to burn my lips, make my heart soar. I tremble from overwhelming joy. I can almost feel the feather pulsating in the notebook. It most definitely wasn't a pigeon.

Ben pulls in his tongue, along with his candy. I confiscate the tin from his pocket. He doesn't stop me from doing so.

He doesn't look at me. He buttons up his jacket, clears his throat, and leaves.

Louise stares at me, intensely, from under her square bob. "Your voice . . . It was . . ."

No hint of boredom now between her lashes. Almost envy instead. I feel all-powerful. My turn for paradise! I shove a whole handful of Ben's candies into my mouth. I stop myself from spitting them back out. I crunch, but don't understand.

Paradise tastes of nothing.

Iris

I laugh. Not too loudly, or too shrilly, or too soon, or too late. My voice blends in with those of the other girls in the class. Perfect timing. I didn't even listen to the joke. No need to: I know instinctively when to open my mouth and when to shut it. We're coming back from the gym. For two hours, my panties have been wedged in my butt; it would take just a second to sort out, a finger quickly slipped under my shorts, but I won't do it. Never in front of the others.

We had volleyball this afternoon and I nailed it. Team sports, they're the most treacherous. Quietly keeping to your position, sending the ball where it's expected, playing as predictably as possible, marking without drawing attention to yourself, not too often, but a little all the same. The worst is serving. All that expectant attention. All those eyeballs glued to me. Last week, a girl messed up her serves spectacularly, one by one, without exception; since then, no one has spoken to her.

Yup, I nailed it, even with elastic digging into my butt.

We walk up the stairs, now grimy after all those rain-sodden shoes. The jokes and laughter stop. Émile. We're going up, he's going down. I look away, like I do whenever our paths cross, like on the day I tried my utmost not to watch what I try my utmost not to remember.

"Pervert."

That's what the girls in my class say to him, one after the

other, as they pass him. It's what I say to him, too. I hang my head to avoid his. The legs sticking up from his socks shock me. Have they always been that skinny? I walk up with my class, he walks down with his. Soon, there'll be much more than stairs between him and me. One girl comes out with a dirty joke, to do with Émile, which I laugh at, not too loudly, or too shrilly, or too soon, or too late. I stare at my sneakers, the same ones the whole gang wears, half-unlaced, just as they're meant to be worn Here. It's only once in our classroom that I finally raise my head, maybe because I know that in here, between these four walls, there's no Émile.

I see the impossible.

Our windows are all different sizes. Some are so narrow a finger wouldn't fit through them. The desks have nothing rectangular about them anymore: they're twisted lozenges, flattened, perched on absurd legs, either too close, or too wide apart. The board, and everything written on it, has been so compressed that it's now just an illegible ribbon. And there are the blobs. Moving blobs, a hideous muddle of profiles and faces, teeth and complexions; it takes me a moment to get that these blobs, they're my classmates. I can't join them. I can't move forward. There's no more space in front, behind, inside, around. The world has lost all depth. No. It's me who's lost all perspective.

I can only see in two dimensions now.

I close my eyes. Reopen them. I see in three again.

I sit on my chair. I laugh with the others. No one picked up on my panic. The rain pounds as hard as my heart. Calm down. Whatever happened, it's over, well and truly over. All the same, I was scared, really scared; not from having seen what I never should've seen; not from going almost blind; no, I was scared, really scared that someone would notice,

scared that a teacher would tell my mother about it, scared
an appointment would be made for me with the optician,
and scared, really scared of becoming the only girl in the class
who had to wear glasses. That, well, it would've been worse
than Émile's skinny legs.

Pierre

He's there. In my place.

I make my way through the classroom, without a kick in the balls or a slap on the ass, until I get to the very back of the back, behind the last row, where the teachers' eyes never go. To my desk.

He watches me. While sitting in my chair.

"It's funny," he says. "It hasn't stopped edging backwards."

He's speaking to me. To me. I'm reeling. What's gone on Here, while I've been away?

He pulls out the chair beside him, a chair that wasn't there before. Reluctantly, I accept the offer. He has a broad forehead, jaw, brow, smile. Skin that's supple and almost poreless. I'm discovering him from the front. From the back, I already know him: very upright, very wide, half-fat, half-muscle, white shirts with spotless collars, and a nape as trim as a lawn. He's one of the twenty-six and is called Vincent.

"Now you're here," he asks, "will it stop edging back?"

And that's when I twig: I, myself, have become one of the twenty-six. I scan the class for Jérémie's back, knowing full well I won't find it. Even his desk has disappeared.

"His family won't send him back to school," says Vincent. "Not after the whole bottle-in-eye thing."

He rolls up his shirtsleeves with care, just long enough to show me his arms. Bruises, lumps, sores, burns, blisters. The works. His fingernails, though, are super clean.

"They didn't hang around, hey?" he says, laughing. "I was the odd one during your suspension. Obviously, before, I sat beside Jérémie, but I'm not going to lie: I won't miss him. Welcome back among us, Pierre. Taking the blame like that, for the class, took balls."

Pierre. I try to swallow, but my throat's gone all dry. I'm one of the twenty-six. I have a name again. I'll be able to take a piss in the regular bathrooms, no more toilets from hell. I'm going to share my desk with another person.

Not only the desk. As the day goes by, Vincent shares everything: the lessons I've missed, the compass I've forgotten, his fries in the cafeteria, the bench during recess, the porn comic, more amusing than arousing, that he pinched from an uncle, and even his umbrella, a real, classy grown-up's brolly, for us to cross the schoolyard in the downpour. And from me, neither a shit nor a shucks; I'm in shock. Even my parents, they've not shared a thing for ages: nothing between them, nothing with me. When they were summoned Here, following the incident, and the principal explained to them that it meant suspension, they didn't share a sigh, either. No one was fooled. They'd all realized that it wasn't really me who'd smashed the bottle in Jérémie's eye, and that, indeed, the bottle was never found, but hey, whatever, to keep up appearances, ten days of lying low and a small check, on the q.t.

"What's that?"

It took me lots of throat-clearing finally to spit it out. Classes are over, everyone's gathering up their stuff, including Vincent. I indicate his little black case. He always drags it around with him everywhere, as well as his bag, but never opens it. I'd already noticed it, that case, when Vincent was just a back to me. Thing is, out of my twenty-six classmates, he's the one I was least curious about. Too placid, too passive, too aloof. Not the type to rough me up, with the other hotheads. So, whatever he's hiding from us in his case, basically, I couldn't give a shit. I'm just vaguely aware that, after all he's shared with me today, from the desk to the umbrella, I can't just leave like that, without a word, and then do the same again tomorrow.

I have to get to the bottom of something before deciding something else, except I don't yet know what.

Vincent looks surprised by my question, in a good way. Jérémie must never have asked him.

"You don't have a bus to catch right away?"

I shake my head in a half-yes half-no kinda way. There are buses every fifteen minutes. Never seen Vincent on a bus, now I think of it.

"Okay, come with me."

I follow Vincent through the school corridors. We're walking against the flow of all the kids getting the hell out, and I feel it in my gut, too, that urgency to turn right around, warning me that hanging out Here after the last bell means risking being trapped for ever. Vincent looks for a quiet corner for us. He drags me into the cleaner's storeroom, and there, in the middle of the carts and cupboards, he goes quiet. I go quiet, too. It stinks of bleach. We wait for the racket of feet to stop being a racket. For the voices to stop being voices. For there to be plenty of space, plenty of silence between the others and us.

Vincent opens his case. Inside, velvet. On the velvet, bits and bobs of wood and metal, which he assembles like pieces of a puzzle.

"A clarinet?"

"An oboe."

He shows me some weird little strips.

"Double reed. Not the same embouchure. Not the same sound."

He moistens his double reed with his lips, and I can't help feeling embarrassed, as though witnessing something very intimate. He broadens his shoulders, blows into the oboe, wiggles his fingers from top to bottom, then from bottom to top; warms the instrument up.

Then he plays.

With my butt on an upturned bucket, I'm even more hunched than ever. My very first thought is: *let's hope it's not long*. The sound is strange. A bit nasal. I'm too close, it's pressing on my eardrums. It's not the kind of music I'm used to listening to. It's not a wall I can forget myself behind. No, that sound, it cracks me, it seeps into me from all directions, through the ears, the eyes, the throat, and even the spine, and at first, it's ugly, and then it's beautiful. Right when I'm thinking I never want it to stop, it stops.

Vincent observes me. Again. His eyes search through my bangs, I escape them as best I can.

"I played. You listened to me. We're friends."

I hold it in. When he dismantles his oboe, I hold it in. When we rush before the gate's closed, I hold it in. It's only once I'm at the back of the bus, facing away from the late-afternoon crowd, that I let myself go and sob. Because Vincent's right. Because he's my first friend. And because I'm going to have to get rid of him.

I'm the odd number, the jack of spades, the lousy kid, and no one can take that away from me. Not even him.

Guy

"Gotta talk about the collection."

The foreign girl looks at me from over her textbook and under her eyebrow. I'd swatted her tray—peas flying everywhere—and as usual, no fear, no sudden start, just her placidly gazing from her book to my face, as if I was the logical continuation of her reading.

"You dodged the first one because, well, you're new, and we don't tax newbies straight off. But that's over, that is. Tomorrow's the second collection and you'll pay up like the rest: banknotes, jewelry, whatever you like as long as it's shiny. This time, no messing with me. Gottit?"

The foreign girl has this fucking annoying way of staring straight at me. In private, between corridors, fine, I've got used to it, but here, right in the cafeteria, in front of every class, in front of the prince himself (even if he doesn't give a shit), it really gets me pissed. She didn't sit at the Bottoms' table, she helped herself to bread three times, she took the last chocolate mousse, the very last! And here she is, studying god knows what, right here, in front of the whole school, between one forkful and the next. She's got no manners. She almost never comes to the cafeteria, but when she does turn up, I get all the Tops on my table baiting me.

Gotta show her who's boss, once and for all.

"Sit down," she goes to me.

She offers me the chair beside her. I remain standing.

"You're my Bottom. I'm your Top. The only table we share's the desk in class."

"As you like."

She speaks so quiet, I can barely hear her. In the cafeteria, it's shouting and screaming, always and everywhere. The foreign girl places her bag on her knees and slips me the latest worksheets. The Tops' table is far away, the prince's one even further; I really hope they think it's me screwing her homework off her, not her correcting mine.

She's covered my work in red marks, neat crossings-out and double underlinings. I feel humiliated.

"I've had enough, I quit."

She looks at me.

"No kidding," I tell her. "Does my head in. I quit."

She looks at me. Just like she looked at me the first day, when she went and stuck an "equals" sign right between my name and hers—a name I've yet to say—and I realize, with a shock, that I'm starting to get used to that eyebrow of hers.

"Any case, I've never understood any of it."

"You've never listened, more to the point. Why not?"

Really serious, her question. Almost . . . what's that word again? *Concerned.* I'm about to snap back that she can mind her own ass, do my homework for me, and sort my crib sheets, like all the other Bottoms do for all the other Tops.

But I say:

"Because there's no point."

I don't know where that came from, didn't even know I thought that, but now, it's blindingly obvious. The classes, teachers, worksheets, notes, it's just hot air. What's really real is my dad on the road day and night, it's my mom cleaning off fly specks in the homes of the rich, a life sentence of exhaustion, so, yeah, if I get the chance, Here, of being almost someone because it's written on a board on the fourth floor, even if I don't know who by, I'm not going to do myself out of making the most of it.

Because it won't last. Because nothing ever lasts.

"You, me, that. I quit. I don't want any learning support. I want what's owed to me."

There's one of those sudden silences in the cafeteria. The prince has just got up. No one hollering anymore, no one eating anymore. When the prince has finished, everyone's finished, whatever class you're in. It's the rule. You put down your cutlery, spit out what's in your mouth, and tough shit if you're still hungry.

The prince is leaving.

We all make sure to lower our eyes. Even the guy clearing the prince's tray away, bet his are glued to the floor. The prince's new high-tops squeak. Looking directly at him is forbidden. He walks slowly. Even slower as he passes behind me. I stand there, squinting at the foreign girl's peas I scattered over the floor, making myself as small as I can, but it's as if I'm still growing right then, right there, in my sweats, in this cafeteria, and I'm far too tall and the prince is far too slow.

He stops. Right behind me. No. Right behind the foreign girl.

I risk a quick glance. Not at the prince, at her. She's not looking at him. It's worse than that. She's wolfing down her chocolate mousse, like nothing's happened. The clicks of her spoon against her teeth are deafening to me.

The prince's high-tops start squeaking again. They move off. They're gone.

Everyone clears away their trays, and beats it, everyone except the foreign girl, who's scraping the bottom of the pot and has even gained a chocolate moustache. It's obvious to me now. Tomorrow, she won't pay her share at the collection. And like all those who don't pay, she'll end the week with her fingers broken, one finger for each spoonful of chocolate mousse. And I won't lift even my littlest finger to help her.

"Too nice, too stupid," I blurt out.

"Guy."

No girl in the school has ever called me by my name. No boy, either. There's something in the foreign girl's eyes, a thing that disturbs me, and it's not about the eyebrow.

"You're not stupid. And you don't need learning support. If you change your mind, I'll teach you to listen."

Emptiness in my head. Emptiness all afternoon. Emptiness in chemistry. Emptiness in history. Emptiness in geometry. Emptiness in my dad's taxi, emptiness under the seat belt, emptiness on my chair at supper. Emptiness in my bed all night.

I am up . . . alarm goes off. I check my homework again, under the light of my bedside lamp. I look at the marking more closely: all my mistakes crossed out in red and, in the margin, dense handwriting explaining where, how, and why I've messed up.

What the hell is it, that thing in her eyes?

Dad drops me off late at the gate. Don't know if he sensed something weird about me, or if it's him who's bushed, but for once, his rearview mirror left me in peace. I climb up the four flights of stairs. I'm shattered, but I take all my time. It's inside me that I feel like I'm climbing.

I arrive outside my classroom. The pair doing the collection are there. The teacher is, too, but he's pretending to search for papers in his bag so as not to see our dodgy dealing.

61

"Hey, dickhead, we've got a problem."

I go up to them. I already know what these two Tops, doing the collection, are going to say to me.

"Your Bottom, y'know, the foreign girl?"

"She didn't pay her share."

"She said 'No thanks' to us."

"You were supposed to explain it to her."

"It's so damn annoying. We'll have to thrash her for you."

"Don't come whining when she's out of service."

The teacher's rummaging so deep in his bag he's suffocating.

I look through the half-open door of the classroom. She's there, sitting at our desk, right-hand row, close to the window. She's already scribbling like crazy in her notebook and the class hasn't even started.

I stuff all my allowance into the collection basket.

"Here's her share," I say. "She's not a foreign girl anymore, now."

I go into class. I sit at my place. Beside her. She looks at me. That thing, in her eyes, I still don't know what it is; but I sure want to.

"Hi Sofie."

The Top-Secret Club

Number One: "I declare this meeting open. Since recess can't be extended, let's try to be efficient and share our observations promptly. Number Two?"

Number Two: "Some schmoil is always discharged on Thursday, always at 2:28 P.M., always in the school's rear gutter."

Number One: "And?"

Number Two: "And it still produces the same effect. I took a sample before it was flushed down the drain. Found myself laughing hysterically, all alone like an idiot, so much my belly ached."

Number One: "Every time?"

Number Two: "Every time, fuck's sake."

Number One: "Perfect. Thanks, Number Two. We thus have confirmation that that day and that time are of crucial importance. So, every Thursday, at 2:28 P.M., an *intramural distortion of the field of reality* takes place Here. The question is: are other phenomena observable elsewhere at that exact moment of the week? Number Four?"

Number Three: "Carry on, just forget me. Not like I'm not used to it."

Number Four: "Nothing to report in the science lab, the gym, and the tech room."

Number One: "And the recording device?"

Number Four: "Just the usual noises. Nothing abnormal."

Number One: "Right. Number Five?"

Number Three: "Bunch of assholes."

Number Five: "Nothing to report in the art studio, the study room, and the music room. Nothing on the recorder."

Number One: "Right. Number Six?"

Number Three: "To hell with you."

Number Six: "Nothing to report in room 3C."

Number One: "That's it? Only room 3C? Why room 3C?"

Number Six: "Because that's where I have classes. It's all very well, you know, your observation missions, your *intramural distortion of the field of reality*, your end of the world, all that, but me, on Thursdays at 2:28 P.M., I'm in class. I can't just cut."

Number One: "We all have classes, Number Six. I know it's not easy, but you must find an excuse to slip away. There are many locations to investigate Here, and a single margin of time each week to do so. There are few enough of us already, and even fewer since the departure of Number Three . . ."

Number Three: "Fuck off."

Number One: " . . . so it's essential that we all join forces. Say you've got a nosebleed, or are desperate to take a piss: the cause is more important than our dignity."

Number Six: "It's easy for you to say: your dad's a teacher, all the teachers favor you. And anyhow, first of all, what have you actually observed, yourself?"

Number One: "The restrooms on the fourth floor, then the principal's office the following week, then the detention room the week after that. Because you see, Number Six, when you're found somewhere you shouldn't be, teacher dad or not, you get a detention and two hundred math problems. And before you ask me: I myself didn't observe anything or record anything, either. But I'm faithful to the cause and

I'll be back on the case next Thursday at 2:28 P.M. And the following Thursday. Until I find a new manifestation of the *intramural distortion of the field of reality*, and a solution to the end of the world."

Number Two: "Me too."

Number Four: "Me too."

Number Five: "Me too."

Number Six: "Okay, okay, me too."

Number One: "There's the bell. I declare this meeting closed."

Number Three: "That's right, go on, get lost all of you. Back to your cameras, your bugging devices, your samples, your microscopes. You observe everything but see nothing. And the more it's under your nose, the less you see it. Nothing to report, hey? Me, I've got tons of thingies to report, thingies to come. Thingies constantly evolving. A disappearance. A murder. A birth. A revolution. But hey, sniffing schmoil, that's fine, too. Jerks."

Second Term

Iris

I'm squashed. My siblings are messing around and singing and blubbing and whining. The backseat of the car's far
too small for them and me (not for us, there's never been
an us). Half-sister: I don't feel even half that right now. The
windows are all steamed up, the heating's on too high, my
bag's heavy on my knees. Everyone shouts, no one speaks.
All I can see of Mom is a slumped shoulder, a stray strand
of hair she gave up tucking behind her ear years ago, and a
limp hand on the steering wheel, as if not really holding it,
but which she occasionally slams on the horn in a fist with
a violence that makes my stomach lurch.

Ingrid is sitting up front. Seniority rights. Much as I hurry
to grow up, there's always that gap that's never filled between
her and me (not us, either), the gap in the increasingly short
and incomplete sentences we reluctantly blurt at each other,
the gap between our hands since she dropped mine, a gap
that already existed before that first day at school (thanks,
Dad) and that my sister does her worst to fill, with her endless friends and fooling around, her bubblegum bursting
onto her face, and that unbearable laugh you can hear at
the other end of town. I'm terrified of becoming as trashy
as her, so I make myself small at the end of the backseat,
like I make myself small on my stool at every meal, like I
make myself small on the sofa that becomes my bed at night,
when the stepfather finally turns off the TV, joins Mom next

door, and gets busy cooking me up some new half-brothers. I make myself small and I wait.

The gate, at last.

Mom brakes, barely long enough for my sister and me to get out and slam our doors, front and back, then Mom's off again without a word, to dump her other brats over there, at my old school, that lost paradise where everything seemed shiny.

Some things do shine Here, too. Invitation cards, for example.

When I enter the classroom, a freezing flight of stairs later, all the girls have got one. They've huddled together around the radiator to warm their butts. There's chortling, there's chirping. I throw them a vague "Hi!", which is vaguely returned. I play it cool as I unzip my puffer jacket; same brand, same color as theirs. But my heart's in my boots. What's this invitation about? Why have they each got one and not me? I do what I do best. I watch, I listen, and I get it. Saturday is Coralie's birthday. She's organized a party. She got the invites printed by a pro, if you please: silk-finish paper, embossed gilding, and even VIP written in big capitals. Fake classy, in other words.

The bell goes.

Why not me? I keep going over and over this question during the class. I observe my neighbor, who's placed her invitation card in full view between us, on the desk, and note that it's encroaching on my territory. Provocation? Why her and not me? She's no slimmer, her figure's no better than mine. I've done everything, absolutely everything, to be one of them. I merged into the crowd, tainted to the bone. I betrayed Émile for them. I even took up smoking. Where, when did I put a foot wrong? I mull it over. It's not the first time. Now I think about it, in sports, they pass to me less and less. And the other day, in the bathrooms, when we drew lots to decide who'd swallow the chewing gum spat out by the prince from the fourth floor, I'd won and then another girl got to do it. I didn't make a fuss, because I didn't want to be a pain and, to be honest, I found it gross, what with my sister already sticking her gum around the apartment, but all the same, the prince's chewing gum, it should've been mine.

I get it. That's it. I should've objected. I lost their respect.

Today's Thursday, the birthday's on Saturday. All's not yet lost. During recess, after the cafeteria, I can't hold back any longer. I confront Coralie, who's vaping under the shelter, behind the backs of the supervisors.

"Gotta light?"

Coralie's lashes are XXL. She flutters them at me for ages, looking astonished, as if she's been searching all over for me, except for where I am. She still flicks on her lighter, and I dip my cig into the flame. I'm trembling, I hope she thinks it's from the cold.

"Thanks."

I'm faking it. With the cigarette. With the smile. But this time, no way am I laying low.

"Happy birthday."

"Sorry?"

Does a good impression of being baffled, Coralie. We're dressed the same, and I suddenly wonder if I, too, look like a kid disguised as a woman.

"I'm just wishing you the best while I can," I say. "I'll think of you on Saturday."

"Didn't I give you an invite?"

"No."

"Shit, hang on. Here. Sorry."

She's stammering, but I can tell she's more confused than embarrassed, and I, who gets everything, well right now, I don't get it. In my fingers, the letters VIP gleam. It's a bit too easy. I got it wrong: it's not their respect I lost, but if not that, then what? It really doesn't matter. I've got what does matter: the same gilded rectangle as the others, which I, too, can display on the desk. I don't really feel like going to this birthday party, but that's not the point. It's about fitting in.

We head back to class. Our noses are dripping. We reek of stale smoke, we're late, the clock says it's 2:27 P.M.; the teacher frowns behind his glasses, but says nothing. They never say anything.

We sit down. Each in our own place, me in mine.

2:28 P.M.

The teacher takes afternoon attendance. Muffled voices. He skips over my name. At first, I don't care—I've got my invitation card, that's enough, I'm not going to draw attention to myself now—but then I think that if I'm marked absent, my parents will be called, and it'll be a whole thing.

I put my hand up.

The teacher has begun the lesson, he's writing on the board. He doesn't see me.

"Sir."

He doesn't turn around.

"You forgot me. In attendance."

He doesn't turn around.

"Sir?"

He turns around. Except he doesn't see me. I put my hand down. I look at the others; I look at Coralie; I look at my neighbor.

And I get it. No one can see me anymore.

Pierre

"Would you like to play?"

Vincent's lips have left his oboe to smile at me. Almost too big for his face, that smile, and yet he's got jaw to spare.

"On yours?"

"No, not mine."

"I don't have an oboe."

"Not necessarily the oboe. Any instrument. Just play one."

"Dunno. Don't think so. Why?"

"We could form a duo, you and me."

I can feel my ears burning, and the boiler's not to blame. We're hiding in the cleaner's storeroom (we've not yet come across a cleaning lady—or cleaning man, either (do they ever clean Here?)): in any case, the storeroom isn't heated.

I scratch my throat.

"I'm not like you."

"Like me in what way?"

"Gifted."

Vincent's smile stretches like an elastic band, so much so, you wonder if it won't finally snap in his face. He's already dismantling his oboe.

"The acoustics really aren't great. Too much concrete. Blowing into it makes me dizzy."

I shrug my shoulders, as if I don't care, but I don't not care at all. Vincent plays for ten minutes a day, after classes are over and before the gate's closed. He plays only for me.

For those ten minutes, everything stops in my head, in my belly, in the bones of my back. I'm no more than a sound that rises to the high notes and descends to the low ones. Ten minutes when I feel at fault for nothing.

We part on the pavement, as usual, and as usual, I dive into the bus, trying to crush as few toes as possible. Vincent doesn't take the bus with me because he goes to the conservatoire, next door. I didn't even know we had a conservatoire next door. Vincent keeps badgering me to come and have a listen, and today I almost said yes; stopped myself just in time.

I mustn't.

I mustn't listen to Vincent's oboe because every time I listen to it, I tell myself "not today" and there've already been far too many "not today"s.

I hunch up.

I get off. I change bus at the town hall. Night's falling faster and faster, darker and darker; the windows become black mirrors that I avoid as best I can. Almost miss my stop. I drag myself through the residential neighborhood. I'm snooty towards equally snooty dogs yapping behind wrought-iron railings. I reach my folks' house. Two windows are lit up, through the blinds: room on the right (my mother), room on the left (my father.) When I walk in, the sitting room's plunged in darkness. I don't switch the light on. I can hear a voice talking on the phone somewhere to the right, the sound of a TV somewhere to the left. I pour myself a giant bowl of cereal, by the blue light of the fridge, and shut myself away in my room, somewhere in the middle.

I hunch up.

Above all, don't think. Above all, don't anticipate.

I think and anticipate all night long.

"You know what goes well with the oboe?"

Vincent comes straight out with his question as soon as I join him at the very back of the classroom. It's morning, it's early, it's bitterly cold, barely a hint of sun, hardly anyone there yet.

"The piano," he answers. "And the violin. And the bassoon. And the flute. I've got plenty of sheet music, you're spoilt for choice."

I scratch my throat.

"Music's your thing."

"It's everyone's thing."

Vincent has really small eyes, but how bright they are! Feel like I've got headlights shining straight at my face. He wants, really wants, to lure me into his world, and I want, really want, to let him. My folks will sign any checks I ask for, and the conservatoire, well, they can definitely afford it. Would it be like another Here? With other odd ones? Other toilets from hell?

I hunch up.

"We'll talk about it after," I say.

The others arrive. The twenty-four others. And with them, the mayhem. They insult each other, fight each other, look for each other, find each other. It starts to ramp up. The teachers spend their lessons separating bodies, sometimes catching a fist themselves. No one can stand anyone anymore. From hostility to the hospital, is just one step. They've all forgotten Jérémie, and every day, I expect another bottle to appear to smash into another head. We never really got along that well, sure, but something kept things from blowing up in all directions like this.

And that something was me.

I hunch up.

Vincent hums right through trig. The hatred festering in the class has no effect on him. He's an island, Vincent, always has been; pacifism in flesh and bone, but mainly flesh. Separately, we're odd ones. Together, we're nothing. I'm nothing.

I decide: today. I wait for the last bell. I clear my throat.

"About what you were saying yesterday. The acoustics. I know of a better hideout."

Vincent's eyebrows shoot up, gleefully.

"I'll follow you."

He follows me: to where I haven't been since the day of the bottle, to the furthest reaches of the school, behind the sports grounds; where no student, no teacher ventures without having been specifically asked to; where Vincent has realized I'm taking him, but still, he follows me, smile on lips, oboe case in hand. I'm hit by the stench before even seeing the toilets from hell. A small graffiti-covered shack in the middle of the brambles. Vincent comes in after me. His polished shoes jar on the filthy floor tiles. He's too fly for a place like this.

I hunch up.

Only two doors in the toilets from hell, and on one, an Out of Order sign. I've never checked what's behind that door. Don't need to. I know—everyone knows—what's there. The worst, in condensed form.

I open it.

Instead of the toilet, a hole in the ground. A putrid pit. Darker than my old folks' sitting room. Darker than Vincent's dilated students. He doesn't run. He says nothing. He smiles. His hand shakes on his oboe case.

Not a word when I push him into the pit.

I'm the odd number, the jack of spades, the lousy kid, and no one can take that away from me.

Madeleine

A few timid little knocks. I say nothing, don't invite in. The door always ends up opening and through it comes a hesitant expression, between expectation and temptation, hope and apprehension, eyes squinting in the shadowy light, until they land on me and, unfailingly, widen: not so much to see more as to take in the profusion of elements that make up the sanctuary. I'm seated in the middle of a heap of multicolored coats, from fake fur to fake leather, and there isn't a centimeter not adorned with a badge, a brooch, a patch, a sticker, a lapel pin, a plastic pearl, a clothes peg, or a chain of paperclips. A rainbow in solid form. A multidimensional rose window. My sanctuary.

This morning, the wide eyes before me are Marwan's. He closes the door behind him, almost reluctantly, and is awkward as he kneels in front of me on the coats, on the patch that's most crumpled, where all the other knees have been before.

"I would like—"

"The color first."

"Oh, yeah. Sorry. Here."

He fumbles in a pocket and then, on a jacket sleeve, somewhere between him and me, sticks a canary-yellow barrette. Not his own, obviously.

"Is that enough for you?"

"It's not for me. It's for That."

77

I don't move an inch, but Marwan's eyes are naturally drawn to the feather attached around my neck.

"I would like—"

"Throw away what is impure."

Marwan's eyes widen even more.

"How do you know—"

"Throw it away."

I indicate the trash can to his left, which is overflowing with half-full packs of cigarettes and unopened cans of beer. He rummages in another pocket. Wood glue. Probably filched from shop. While he puts it in the trash, I feel sorry for what brain cells he has left.

"You're great."

"Not me. That. What do you want?"

Marwan's eyes suddenly narrow and dart away, in search of some other object to focus on. He won't find one. Room 1 hasn't always been a sanctuary. Before, it was called "the cellar." Accessible only from the rear of the school, beyond the bike and scooter sheds. Fungi on the walls. A single window coughing up a dusty light. Beaten earth under the chairs and desks. Classes haven't been held here for decades.

"I would like normal skin."

I thought as much. Marwan's cheeks are a disaster zone. Craters and bumps: like being on the Moon.

"That's your request?"

"I reckoned that . . . since all the pimples you had have gone . . ."

I refrain from saying they're not all that's gone. Periods, too. And sweat. And cavities. And other things I had to give up. In their place, I'm entitled to a mocking snigger from Louise whenever I use recess to collect my thoughts in the sanctuary. In class, we barely talk to each other anymore. Because I was Chosen and not her.

"You'll help me, hey? You helped the others."

"It's not me who helps. It's That."

Marwan shivers. I wonder whether it's from fear. My skin no longer tells me when it's cold. I don't know if the coats under us are comfortable, or give that illusion, but anyhow, that's not essential.

I remove the pendant from around my neck.

"You've washed your hands?"

"Three times."

I hand the feather to Marwan, who takes it with the tips of his fingernails (nice and clean, I must admit) for fear of damaging it. And suffering the consequences.

"What must I do?"

"Nothing. It's That that'll do."

"Should I pray?"

"Unimportant."

"I'll pray in my head. Just in case."

He closes his eyes tight enough to tangle his lashes. His face tenses up, his lips mutter. He's rushing too much. He's thinking too much. Of the recess he's missing; of the imminent bell; of the fear of being late; of pimples; of his life; of death. And like all those who come to consult me in the sanctuary, he begins to slow down, to soften. He's not praying anymore. I see his entire skin relaxing. I contemplate the pustules rising from it, some about to burst spontaneously. Had something similar myself: a restrictive and annoying body. That was before the Voice. The very Voice that's rising in my throat:

"In The Schoolyard. Under The Clock. At The Foot Of The Wall. Where The Tarmac Is Cracked. Eat The Soil."

Marwan opens his eyes. Gives me back the feather.

"Okay."

He stands up. Soon his acne will be cured. As were Clara's gastritis, Ben's cold sores, Sylvie's sprain, and Julien's melancholy. And as Marwan closes the door, and I return to my meditation, a thought assails me—what I am, what I'm becoming, me without Louise, what I was Chosen for, with the capital C, thanks to That—which I quash immediately with a fervent pinch of the thigh, even though I no longer feel pain.

Shit, that can't be all.

Guy

I strut around the corridors, cut jerks. Fists in pockets, lashes crusty from the cold, roll-neck unrolled up to my nose, but ears well out in the air. I've put my beanie on the back of my head, so it makes them stick out even more.

Learning to listen.

I listen. To the wets, the prats, the posers, the twits, the supervisors, the teachers, wherever tongues are wagging. I'd never paid attention to how much gossip goes on in school. On the benches, under the shelter, in the bathrooms, between staircases, even in class, especially in class, it never stops. All these years, I only thought about what I should say so as not to seem like a moron to the other Tops; even if I did screw it up every time. As for listening, it drains me even more. As if I was filling myself with everyone's thoughts, except mine. Since I've been listening, I hear a bit of everything, a lot of nothing, and more and more it makes me feel full, less and less like myself, and I'm not so sure I love that.

But hey, there you go: Sofie.

I'm lurking outside the principal's office. The door's slightly ajar and there's some serious yakking going on inside. Some guys are asking questions. Cops. The principal gives them the smile treatment as he hands them a paper.

"The attendance sheet. You see? His name was ticked right up to the last hour. He left with the others after the class. If something did . . . happen . . . it's very regrettable, obviously, but it wasn't here with us. Have you enquired at the conservatoire?"

The principal spots me outside his door. He's not smiling at all now.

"You don't have a class, young man?"

I shrug one shoulder; my bag's weighing the other one down.

"The teacher's not there, Sir. He's got flu. Something like that."

My voice is sucked in by my roll-neck.

"No reason to hang around the corridors. Go off to . . ."

The principal doesn't finish his sentence. He's remembered that I'm a Top, not a mega popular Top, sure, but a Top all the same, and Tops, well, they don't get sent to the study room. He vaguely indicates to me to get lost anyway. The cops stare at me, stare at him, stare back at me.

I scoot.

Barely three steps and I slam on the brakes, just in time to avoid crashing into the prince, coming towards me. I make sure to look straight down at the floor, at the black and white (black and gray) tiles of the corridor. The prince brushes past me, he smells of dope.

"Hi," I say.

For him, I did roll down my roll-neck. He doesn't respond, he never responds, but his nose makes a noise I recognize, the very one all the Tops' noses make at every collection, when I pay Sofie's share out of my own pocket, a noise I hate to listen to, but I listen to all the same, a very brief expelling of air, as if they were determined not to breathe in mine. But me, I do breathe in the prince's air, and it gives me a kind of jolt inside.

I raise my eyes.

Not that high, you know, the eyes, not up to the prince's eyes, but I still catch his legs moving off, his forever-new shoes, his jewelry tied onto both laces, his jeans ripped under one bun, like all jeans have to be Here, even when it's shit cold, his silver-ringed hand holding the smoking joint, not even trying to hide it, and who gives a fuck if there are cops nearby. All the booty from the collections: on the prince.

My heart's racing. From bravado, or fear, or shame, I'm not really sure.

I go into the library. What they call the library. Trashed books, rickety tables, pathos in poster form, and a defunct percolator: in short, the dumping ground for stuff no one wants anywhere else. Never seen a supervisor or a student around here. Apart from Sofie, obviously.

She's pulled out the chair next to hers. An invitation; I slump onto it. She waits. She waits for me.

I'd rather Sofie didn't know that I pay for her at the collections. Like I'd rather she didn't know all the filthy stories being spread about the two of us. It might be all that stops me losing face in the eyes of the other Tops: all the gross things they think I do to Sofie as soon as it's just me and her. I clear my throat.

"A sub's gonna substitute for a sub. Piercings aren't in anymore, except for navel ones. Some trashy movie showing that's a must-see. A sappy birthday party last Saturday. The juniors have now got a guru squatting in Room 1; supposedly, she can do almost anything. Oh, and there are cops in with the principal. I think it's about the boy who's run away."

Sofie listened to me . . . what's that word again? *Intently*. It's like she touches my words with every inch of her skin, and captures something underlying them, some hidden meaning that completely escapes me. I really don't listen like she does.

"You're making progress."

I wipe my nose on my sleeve.

"Okay. I've disappointed you."

"Why's that?"

"Because that's what I always do."

When she frowns, Sofie's brow looks like a diving bird. And still that thing in her eyes . . . She's wearing mustard mittens I bet she knitted herself. If I didn't pay her share, at the collections, they'd have forced her to eat them, some crap like that.

I'm swinging back on my chair. Aha. On the library ceiling, too, there are the footprints of the upside-down student. What do they all call him again? Théodore? No. Théophile. With a name like that, no way does he actually exist.

"The prince. I looked at him."

Sofie almost smiles at that.

"What did you learn from doing so?"

"Nothing."

"Well, then you can't have really looked at him."

"Eh?"

"If you'd looked at him directly, you would have understood."

"I would have understood what?"

"Why it's forbidden."

I swing harder and harder, faster and faster. Shit. I missed what was important; I always miss things. Teachers' lessons, same thing. I can clean out my ears, but it's like I'm hearing nothing. And my father's lessons, in the taxi, I miss so much, I don't even try to listen anymore.

As for Sofie, she goes straight for what's important. She's

rummaging in my bag; a weird little habit of hers. She digs out the diving goggles.

"You've got swimming."

She's not asking a question. She tweaks the elastic of my bathing cap, the most humiliating invention of all time. Look enough of a dickhead without needing that.

"This afternoon, yup."

"You enjoy it."

Again, not really a question.

"I've never asked myself."

I've never asked Sofie, either. Don't really dare to. Girls who miss sport, usually it's because they're on the rag, but Sofie, she hasn't come once since the start of the year. It's not possible to be permanently on the rag, surely?

I take my bag back from her before she pulls out my trunks. And suddenly, without warning, the cops come right back into my mind.

"There, now," says Sophie, really screwing up her eyes. "You've just made one."

"Made one?"

"A connection. What did you just think about? Right then."

"The start of the year."

"Yes."

"There was this boy in sports. The one who had a bottle smashed in his face."

"Yes."

"I think it's the same class as the boy who's run away."

"Yes."

"And that's it. Just . . . I find that odd. A bit."

"Why do you pay my share at the collection?"

I almost fall over, along with my chair. Sofie's face hasn't changed a bit, but her fingers are fiddling with her pen.

"Let me be perfectly clear," she adds. "I'll never pay a thing. Neither to them, nor to you. I'm not playing that game. But why you, why are you paying my share?"

I don't know what to say. Cos I've never thought about it. Didn't want to think about it. Why *do* I pay her share, Sofie's share, then? Why do I risk my entire reputation for her, this girl who doesn't even do my homework? And how can I have thought she wouldn't notice a thing, Sofie, who notices everything?

I'm too dumb.

"Are you expecting anything in return?" she asks.

Something in return?

Her pen jiggles even more between her fingers, but her eyes, they don't move.

"I expect nothing. I pay, that's all."

I feel really, really dumb. I am really, really dumb. And whoever writes out the pairs for us, on the board on the fourth floor, he's also really, really dumb to have made me a Top, made Sofie a Bottom, because let's admit it once and for all, yeah, it should've been the other way around, and yeah, maybe that is in fact why I pay for her at collections, and I can see now, from the deepening frown on her brow, that Sofie's just realizing that she's wasting her time with me, and that, well, that scares the shit out of me more than the prince does.

But instead, she hits me with:

"I love you."

The Substitute Teacher

I tried. To get them on board. Make them laugh. Make them quake. All day long, I tried. The only raised hands: bathroom, Miss. My fingers are frozen. Heating not working in the classroom, a window not closing properly, and that undrinkable tea I was politely offered in the staff room . . . In short, my first day. The second one, once the students start to feel at ease and test my boundaries, oh yes, the second one will be worse. And yet, tomorrow, I'll try again.

They've all gone now; I lock the classroom door behind me.

I don't take the elevator. I prefer the stairs, one landing after another—returning from a dive, decompression sickness can soon strike. A few straggling students walking around me. Above all, no contact! A teacher, a substitute what's more, you only touch from a distance, lobbing erasers at their back while they're writing on the board. That's the rule. One of their many rules. Mine once, in another life.

Short stop on the second floor. Are they still there? They are. The shoe prints on the ceiling seem really small to me, so distant . . . The upside-down student.

A smile. A memory.

I make some photocopies. The principal leaves his office just as I'm leaving the staff room. Awkward encounter. For him more than me.

"So, your first day? Did it go well?"

He wants to seem jovial, but his feet, already pointing to

the exit, don't lie. The feet never lie. I can tell he's trying to remember my name.

I come to his assistance.

"Thérèse."

"Thérèse, yes. Of course. It's a pleasure to have you back among us. On the other side of the fence."

He switches his attaché case to the other hand.

"I didn't mean to suggest . . . The expression isn't really . . ."

"It's totally appropriate," I say. "I was the taught. Today, I'm the teacher."

He looks at his watch; a very fine watch.

"Well, well, see you tomorrow?"

"See you tomorrow."

I thread my way between colleagues' cars. I don't drive. It's like with the elevator, a need for slowness. And anyhow, I don't have far to go. I cross a few roads, walk up a few floors. The scent of eucalyptus, keeps your chest clear in winter and mosquitoes away in summer. From the balconies of the apartment building, you can see the school. Too much evening: its facades are more gray than yellow. It used to terrify me. I think it still does terrify me a little.

I don't turn the light on in the apartment. Not straight away. Too much evening and too much of me. First the whiff of old toilet paper, first the flatulence of the piping. I drop my bag on the floor, my binders clatter. The kitchen, I know it by touch. I know the sink, I know the gas cooker, I know every cupboard. I empty out the coffee-maker from this morning, the better to fill it. It needs descaling, it's going to splutter all over us.

The phone. That, too, I pick up without looking for it.

"So, the great return?"

The effect of his voice is instant. I'm not cold at all anymore.

"Shocking."

"Tell me."

"Hold on."

I switch on the light. Get rid of my pumps, stockings, skirt, chignon. I wind up on the sofa in my underwear, coffee in one hand, receiver in the other.

"It was like fitting back into a very old skin."

"Ouch. That must hurt."

I twirl my toes in the long cable of the phone. My nail polish shimmers. My leg hair does, too.

"It's mainly that nothing's changed. The schoolyard, the classrooms, the corridors, the students."

"Well, of course. Particularly the students."

I laugh, and it relaxes my whole body. The sofa smells of Gran.

"Of course, the names aren't the same, the faces aren't the same, but yes, they really are the same students. The classes with odd numbers, for example: they still end up with one lousy kid. And then that girl cloistered in Room 1, as if she really is the first to ever go through a mystical phase. On the fourth floor, they've got a prince. Well, we had a queen."

"I bet that was you."

His voice. Even over there, even from afar, it tickles me.

"You're silly. Oh yes! They've formed another Top-Secret Club."

"Funny. We had one of those, too."

"A kid has disappeared."

"Less funny, that. A runaway?"

"They don't know. It was just before I arrived. He was expected at the conservatoire after school, but never turned

89

up. The police came. Asked a few questions. Left. I've got a bad feeling about it. I can't stop thinking of his parents. The horror of uncertainty."

I have a gulp of coffee, tepid already. His voice goes quiet with me. Waits.

"And the footprints on the ceiling, you know?" I continue. "Still there. Nothing's changed since my time. Nothing ever changes, Here. Even Gran's apartment hasn't changed. Everything the same as before, minus Gran."

"Is she okay?"

"I'm visiting her on Sunday. That's the least I can do."

"She's family."

I think of my parents, who gave me the keys to the apartment when they picked me up at the station. *It's the simplest thing.* Simplest for me or for them? I put my cup down on the coffee table. Still lying on it is a crossword puzzle, half-finished in the shaky handwriting of an old lady.

"And you?" I ask.

"I miss you. That too, you see, doesn't change."

I smile. But not for long.

"In fact, the problem Here isn't so much that it doesn't change. It's more that everything starts again. And I'm scared."

"You? Who's braved all the Heres in the country? Who takes over from those who give in? Who plugs in the gaps? Who's forever starting from scratch? What on earth could you be scared of?"

I sigh.

"Of it ending the way it did last time."

Iris

I slurp from my mug at my corner of the table. I made it all by myself: the milk in the pan boiled right over. Not one reproach. Mom cleaned up the mess on automatic pilot, between two bits of toast and three bouts of yelling. My half-siblings swirl around me without touching me. Ingrid keeps chuckling under her mop of hair, which she says is *avant-garde*, repeating it between each mouthful of cereal, as she sits opposite me and her eyes look straight through me. And the stepfather has lost his nasty habit of ruffling, with a small, greasy palm, hair that's taken me over an hour to style.

Invisible.

At the back of the car, invisible. In the corridors at school, invisible. In the middle of the classroom, in lessons, during recess, in the bathrooms, everywhere, all the time, since Thursday afternoon: I am invisible. Teachers' and students' eyes skim over me without ever glimpsing me. Neither my presence, nor my absence is noticed: I see without being seen, I see and I live, I've found what I was always searching for. The blind spot.

I no longer leave the cafeteria starving, after avoiding eating anything that might get stuck in my teeth or shame my chin. I no longer check, obsessively, in the pocket mirror hidden in my make-up bag, whether the burning itch on my lip isn't turning into a purulent monstrosity. I'm no longer haunted by the blood days, waiting for the bell, thighs squeezed together, tummy cramped, terrified at the thought of reaching the bathrooms too late, and discovering on my chair, on my skirt, what I myself have mocked so often with the others, when the accident happens to one of us.

I'm finally relieved of the burden of my own presence. Transparent! Transparent, yes, but cautious.

This invisibility, so hard won, can blow up in my face at any moment. Not won. Given. It's the walls Here, their silent strength: they've given me camouflage. Is it a test? I don't know what, I don't know why, and I really don't care, I just want it to continue. No coughing, no talking, barely moving in gym. I even do my homework, in the evening, in front of the stepfather's too-loud TV. I watch and I listen and I get that, above all, I mustn't deviate from daily imitation, so I reproduce scrupulously, methodically, day after day, the same movements as the others, and, evening after evening, I ignore my family just as much as they, on their side, ignore me.

Until this morning.

In chemistry, I let out a burp that cleaves the air like a thunderbolt. No one bats an eyelid. I hesitate a little, barely, then slip out of the class to have a smoke in the schoolyard. On my return, I notice that the teacher has closed the door. I reopen it. The teacher closes it behind me without a pause in her lesson.

It's as simple, as trivial, as that.

In the next period, I smoke my cig right in the classroom. The one after that, I do a cartwheel. And as I end up bored stiff, in the afternoon I leave to spy on the other classes, click, door open, click, door closed, one floor after another. I linger with a teacher who's a smidgen less tedious than ours;

a substitute, I think. I hang around until the prince's class, for the thrill of breaking another rule. I look directly at the prince. And I get it. And I have fun. I have fun like I haven't had fun since the days in my old schoolyard, the very first one, in that time of unselfconscious games, of my father still being alive, and of Émile's hand, before. I stop having fun. I've done all the classes except his, Émile's, because invisible or not, I want my eyes far away from his.

The bell goes. Right, come on, don't want to miss Mom.

I rush to collect my bag from my classroom, on the first floor. Too late, already locked, never mind. I stick close to the bodies in the corridors, looking for my sister's—hard to miss, that body! Ingrid's pecking all her friends on the cheek in the schoolyard. I can't even remember what it was like, before, having her lips on my cheek; noisy, probably.

She walks through the gate. I can't seem to.

Try as I might to move forward, I'm running on the spot. As if the gate was open for Ingrid and closed for me. Everyone leaves except me, including the last straggler, the last teacher, the last supervisor, my last friends. Beyond the gate, I can see the pavement, the road, the cars. Mom's car. She stops, Ingrid gets in. And on the car door that slams shut—so close, that door! I could almost touch it!—everything is reflected, except me.

Pierre

Twenty-four backs. A sleepy row of hoodies, in single file, in front of the pommel horse. Only big brands. On me, too, only big brands, deliberately big brands, to be sure it all gets swiped later, after the sports class, between two changing-room doors and some slaps, until I'm left with only my boxers and some bruises—my folks will pull out the wallet this evening without asking who, how, or why. Everything's back to normal since . . . Well, everything's back to normal. I'm the odd number, the jack of spades, the lousy kid, and my desk edges back every night.

Right now, it's me edging back. It's even more arctic in the gym than out in the schoolyard. Nothing but cloud through the windows and a kind of cold-gruel light from the grimy bulbs. Thursday weather, in other words.

The teacher's shouting at us between whistle blasts; I don't like that whistle.

"Come on, come on, move your asses over there!"

The bodies, stiff and lanky, launch themselves, one after the other, towards the pommel horse. Whistle. Half-hearted jump, only just gets over. Whistle. The girls yank their hoodies down over their butts before setting off. Whistle. The boys let it all hang out. Whistle. And me, standing back, on the lookout, bent over, I wait for what inevitably happens to one of them: a spectacularly clumsy crash-landing.

And there it is. A clinker, lots of laughter, and anger.

The insults are already flying around. Wouldn't take much more for another bottle to appear from nowhere, and with it another Jérémie, even if everyone's forgotten about Jérémie, just like everyone's forgotten about . . . Well, everyone's forgotten about him, too. Even the cops.

I run like an idiot, don't wait for the whistle, pound the trampoline, jump awkwardly and crash-land as well as I can. Almost bust my schnoz. I take all the jeers, all the shame, don't concede a crumb to those who crash-landed before me, and above all, no, above all don't let any of my satisfaction show—it would spoil theirs. All would be perfect right now if it wasn't for the teacher's whistle. Makes me think of a sour note from an oboe, in the cleaning store, after lessons; I don't like that whistle.

The bell goes.

I get properly fleeced after showering—they don't even leave me my sneakers. I have a change of clothes ready, as usual, carefully selected by me: trousers with suspenders, argyle socks, and cardigan with elbow patches. All that's missing is a sign saying "Hit hard."

As I'm not allowed to use the gym shitters any more than the school ones, I rush off to empty my bladder in the bushes during lunch. I've not been back to the toilets from hell since . . . Well, I just don't go there anymore. As long as I don't go there, it's as if what happened at that pit, and all that preceded it, didn't really matter. As long as I don't go there, he never existed, neither him, nor his smile, even pinched on the oboe, that smile, even while blowing out baroque music, that smile; and even the absence at my desk, when I return to lessons, between the wall and the backs, yes, even that absence doesn't exist.

On the board, an endless stream of polygons, equations,

graphs, abscissas, coordinates, and I fill myself with figures so as not to think about the pit, and when the figures on the board are no longer enough, I add those on my watch.

2:12.

2:17.

2:23.

2:28.

To my left, a chair. On the chair, a profile. On the profile, a smile. Vincent is there. Sitting calmly in his place, as if he's never left it, he's there. His thick hands, smooth and solid, lie perfectly flat on his oboe case. He smells neither of piss, nor of slurry, nor of the pit. He smells of nothing at all; I'm drowning in my own sweat.

I'm not the odd number. I'm not the jack of spades. I'm not the lousy kid. Because if Vincent is really real, if I haven't killed him, then maybe it's me who never existed.

Guy

The windows whine, the door wheezes, a branch of whatever knocks on some glass, *tap, tap,* and I can feel a draft
above my socks strong enough to yank the hairs out. There's
one helluva wind today, and it's shaking up the whole school.
There's slamming, creaking, noise everywhere; everywhere
except between us. In class, no one squeaks. Not because
of the surprise test—tests have never stopped us from running riot: no, this silence is unnatural, and the more I listen
to it, the more I hear nothing. In front of me, behind, all
around, the Bottoms scribble away on their papers—and on
the Tops' papers, too—looking like they'd stick their faces
to them if they could. They stink of fear, a fear I don't get at
all, or rather, don't want to get, and my paper doesn't fill up.
Impossible to get my pen moving in sludge like this.

Shit.

Sofie, beside me, she's already handed hers in. Arms
crossed on the desk, very calm, she's got that look of hers
that's both all outward and all inward. She's listening to the
wind, or to the void, what do I know? I don't ask, don't talk
to her much anymore, in fact, just the bare minimum, hi,
how's it going, no kidding, ciao. So there ain't much noise
between Sofie and me anymore, either, but that silence, no
mystery there, it comes from me.

I look at Arianne, next desk along, who's careful not to
look back at me. Even the Tops are super uneasy.

Shit, shit, shit.

And yet they don't know. They can't know. What happened in the library stayed in the library, and even Sofie, yup, even she, who never does anything the way others do, I don't think for a fucking second she'd have been stupid enough to repeat—and who to, hey, for starters?—what she said to me.

What she never should have said to me.

There are tons of rules here. Too many to make sense of them most of the time. And almost every week, a new rule suddenly hits us, just like that, and we're not sure from who and we're not sure why, but a rule's a rule, we follow it pronto. In short, there's loads of rules here, sure, but among them, there's one that's at the very top of the list, even higher than the Tops themselves, even higher than the rule about not blubbing.

And that rule, Sofie flaunted it. That's not the right word. *Flouted*, that's it.

Here, you can crush on, tease, bed, screw, touch up, talk dirty, jerk off, fuck, and sin all you like, but you never say, ever, for any reason, what Sofie said. My pen's not moving on my paper. I've had something, like, stuck in my throat for days now, and nights, something that just won't go down. It's because Sofie's words, those words, I didn't respond to them. How should I have responded to them, anyhow? How do you respond, eh, to what, above all, must never be said?

"You know the answer."

Sofie whispers almost without moving her lips, her arms still crossed on the table, the look in her eyes as vague and, weirdly, as focused as ever, and it's a serious relief to me, her keeping them well off me right now. The answer to the test, yeah, I know it. We've looked at this math homework together a zillion times before she . . . well, before. It's the pen that doesn't want to. And it's my father who's going to be disappointed again; again and again; again squared; again².

Someone somewhere is tapping on their desk. The sound of rings. The prince.

Suddenly, I get it. The silence, the fear, the sludge, all that, all that: it's him. He's lording it in the middle of the class, but the vibe he's giving off is unfamiliar, impatient, tense, and tense-making; the prince, we only look sidelong at him, and I almost—almost—looked directly at him the other day, the prince, I daren't look at him at all anymore. Same with the teacher. He does the prince's homework for him. And the wind, yeah, the wind, too, it's stirring up the whole class, except for the prince. In short, if everything's tight as a spring this morning, it's gotta be because of the prince.

A punishment's going to be imposed at recess. They're grim, the prince's punishments.

On Monday it was sunny so we all left the cafeteria early, to quickly play some matches between classes in the school-yard. With Karim, our best goalie, we were leading two-nil. Karim's the perfect Top. He's handsome, he's stylish, he's imposing, and when he's in goal, he lets nothing in. Almost nothing. The other side sent him a super sneaky ball, and it wasn't all his fault anyhow, we'd fucked up our defense and, whatever, we still won the match.

But there it was. Karim had lost face. Worse, he'd lost the whole class's face.

The prince, who'd watched it all from his chair, a chair specially positioned in the best spot, well, the prince said nothing. He stood up. We all lowered our eyes. Two hours later, in history class, Karim gets a note. A note from the prince. All that was written was: "Hit yourself." So Karim hit himself. Just like that, in the middle of history. The teacher almost intervened, but then chickened out. Karim hit himself. He hit himself until his face was covered in blood. He hit himself until he passed out. Because the prince's note had asked him to do so.

There. That's what happens when you lose the whole class's face.

That's what's going to happen today to one of us.

The bell goes, the whole class streams out. One of us is going to pay dearly. And it's me. Or Sofie. Or both of us. In any case, it's going to be costly. I tell myself again that it can't be because of what Sofie shouldn't have told me, but if it isn't that . . .

"What's the problem?"

I stare at Sofie's eyebrow to avoid what's going on beneath it. I'd handed in a blank piece of paper and tried to sneak off, but she caught up with me like a shot. For someone who's forever skipping sport, she's some sprinter. No reproach in her question, and yet I'd have preferred that to this fucking curiosity that I know is sincere.

"I'm going for a crap."

I'm only half-lying. My plan is to hide in the fourth-floor bathrooms for as long as it takes, all day if necessary, and, yes, maybe even the following days, so I'm forgotten by the prince, the teachers, my father. And, while I'm at it, Sofie.

Although I charge along the corridor, she runs backwards, to face me. At least there's no one left on this floor, apart from the wind, making all the notices along the wall flutter.

"Is it because of the other day? When I told you I loved you?"

That thing stuck in my throat, even if I don't get what

it is, almost chokes me. It's like that thing in Sofie's eyes: something that's not done for me.

"You're busting my balls."

Sofie stops dead; I do, too. I sink, deep as I can, into my pockets, my sneakers, my hood. Pity's sake, would she quit looking at me, following me, speaking to me, I just want to stop being here, stop being anywhere anymore.

"Guy."

She's not the angry type, Sofie. So steady, her voice, so firm, you could sit on it. I disappoint my parents without having to lift a finger. What have I got to do, for fuck's sake, to disappoint her?

"Don't get the wrong idea," she goes to me. "How I feel concerns only me. I expect nothing in return. And if it made you feel uncomfortable, I'm sorry, I won't mention it anymore. I'll leave you to defecate in peace."

I remain rigid as her little granny steps move off down the corridor, linger in front of the board of pairs, in front of the class's names, our two names, her "equals" sign, before going down the stairs and leaving me alone with the wind.

I head straight to the bathrooms, I bolt the stall door. I'd kept my mouth shut like a real coward. I didn't warn her not to go to the schoolyard, specially not today, specially not with the prince's punishment, but I have to think of myself first, fuck it, even if I can't stand myself anymore, fucking shit, even if Sofie apologized, fucking goddam shit, for saying to me what no one's ever said to me.

I unbolt the door, come out of the stall.

The prince is there. Barely time to realize it's him, and I've dropped my head right down.

He was waiting for me.

"Ah," I go. "The punishment's for me."

I'm surprised at how relieved that makes me I feel. I close my eyes, to avoid looking directly at the prince for a start, but also in anticipation of the punches I'll have to throw at myself as soon as he orders me to. I just would have liked to know why.

"More of a deal."

The prince's voice. Don't know how far back I last heard it, but can't get over how little it's changed since then. And yet it's firmer than Sofie's, that voice. Unbreakable, a voice like that.

I keep my eyes very closed and my ears very open.

"I want us to swap."

"What?"

I can hear the prince breathing. I can smell his dope breath. He's standing up close. Much too close.

"You and me. On the board. In class. I want us to swap places."

Madeleine

I contemplate my Q-tip. Immaculate. I plunge it again into both ears, really deep, twist it one way, then the other. Whiter than white.

It's weird. Weeks ago, I banished from my bathroom all sanitary towels, acne creams, cleansing patches, deodorant, hair remover, shampoo, soap, toothpaste, even toilet paper, and it's made no difference to me. Literally. I considered each stage of my metamorphosis as the logical, even liberating workings of a miraculous mechanism. The end of weight. Light once more, like in the golden age before I was born, before my mother expelled me first from her belly, then from her life.

I felt like I was floating all weekend, nothing but a smooth skin, with nothing inside it or around it.

So why now, on Monday morning, does this Q-tip disturb me so much? I pinch my thigh, a habit I can't seem to drop, even though it increases my frustration. The good thing about the pain was that it balanced out any meanness; without the pain, I have to show myself worthy of It. Unfailingly.

In the mirror, I avoid lingering on the feather hanging between what's left of my breasts. What color should I wear? I don't usually ask myself the question. It knows and It tells me. It loves colors, but It has its preferences.

This morning, It asks nothing of me. Did I hesitate too

long? I pull on a raspberry sweater and hope this choice will redeem me.

"I say, you smell nice."

Grandad is waiting for me at the bottom of the stairs with a basket of croissants and that smile, stuck between awkward lips, he treats me to every morning. I take his word for it: I can no longer smell my own odor (of sanctity?), no more than I can smell that of his aftershave, or of our house, a spruce mix of bleach, laundry detergent, and polish. But I do remember.

The walls of the dining room are sagging under all my drawings, framed by Grandad, hung by Nana, from my first collage in kindergarten to my latest rose window, and a parade of horse profiles in between. I grab the mug waiting for me, scalding or tepid I couldn't say, then bite into a croissant whose crust is flaky I guess, and I suppose soft on the inside, and I chew for show, to give the illusion, before spitting it all out into the toilet. My grandparents pretend as much as me; the sidelong glances they give me are less and less tender, more and more intimidated. They miss the days of markers and pastels. On Sunday, they gave me a box of watercolors, as if that could rekindle the flame, but the problem isn't about the colors. It's about the too-white whiteness of the paper.

About the too-white whiteness of the Q-tip.

"The others are waiting for you."

Gran delicately lifts the curtain at the window. The morning lights up the polish on her nails, the powder on her cheeks, her white eyebrows, far too white. *The others*, for her, are all those who don't have the privilege of being me.

"They don't bother you, at least, those guys?"

"No, Grandad."

"Would you like us to go with you?"

"No, Nana."

On the pavement, the herd stamp their feet. I live in the neighborhood of the school. I don't know how it got out, but I can't leave home anymore without hands shooting out towards me, towards my feather, to a chorus of "Pleeease!" I make my way through the crowd of the faithful. I'm followed, stalked, begged, urged, but not touched, less out of respect for me than out of fear of It. It's only Monday and everyone already wants their miracle. Less greasy, bigger, less flat, smaller, a new nose, new teeth, a different family, more vacations, and lots wanting to lose their virginity, without pain, of course, with someone experienced, preferably.

Generally, I point at two or three of them, randomly, boom, boom, and tell them to come to the sanctuary during the next recess. Not this morning. I walk straight ahead of me, eyes on the ground, counting the dog turds until I reach Here. I walk through the gate. I avoid the people and the pleeeases. I try not to think about the Q-tip, but think about it all the same.

Why did I seek everything, accept everything, take on everything, apart from it?

The bell isn't enough to scatter the supplicants. They harass me between the bikes and scooters in the carpark. Help me, c'mon, you're pushing it, don't be a diva, take my color and work your miracle! The voices stop imploring, become imperious, but the Voice inside me remains silent. It keeps quiet; It has sensed my doubt; It's abandoning me. I regret not being able to sweat anymore, I sure need to.

I dive into Room 1 and lock the door.

"The price of success."

Louise. She's sitting on a desk, legs crossed, indistinct in the murky light. Between her fingers, a cigarette stub

105

splutters smoke. She doesn't throw away what's impure, Louise, she takes it straight out of the trash. First time she's come to the sanctuary. She's clearly rejected the carpet of multicolored coats at the heart of the room; rejected the chairs, too. A rickety desk, that's the imbalance she needs.

"The bell rang. You shouldn't be cutting."

I almost said, "shouldn't be here." Louise is the last person I want to see—want to be seen by—now. She's also the only one in our class never to have asked me for any miracle, and here she is, catching me at my weakest moment.

"It's fine, it's physics, I'm in the teacher's good books," she says. "With my grades, I can get away with being late. But you, too, you're cutting. Are you hiding?"

Why didn't she come on Friday, Louise, before the Q-tip, before all the questioning. Why didn't she come when, finally, I could have shown her that there was something at which I was better than her?

She's smiling; I think she's smiling, it's so dark in here. In any case, she's oozing derision.

"The teachers put up with your little consultations because they benefit, too, but watch out: your grades are in freefall. Seems like miracles can't do everything."

"What are you here for? For a consultation, too? Today, It's seeing no one."

"I couldn't care less about It."

Louise doesn't even look at the feather at my neck. Or at me, either, actually. Her eyes flit around without ever settling anywhere.

"I bet you spent the weekend at Nana'n'Grandad's again. Well, I hung out with high-school boys. And high-school girls, too. They told me I looked much more mature than my age. They let me ride a motorbike. And do other things, too. You can't imagine how hard it was for me to come back here this morning. No, you really can't imagine."

For Louise, it's only elsewhere that she feels alive. For me, it's Here. Here with It and without the others.

She sucks smoke in, snorts it back out again through her nostrils, and adds:

"You smell really nice."

The sun filters through the filthy windows. Shock. The velvetiness, silkiness, and suppleness of Louise have ceased to exist. What confronts me, sitting awkwardly on that desk, is a pockmarked skin stretched over coarse bones, swamped by greasy hair. All that thickness, that unbearable and grimy heaviness that I've gradually rid myself of: now it's Louise who's lumbered with them. Transformed in the space of just one weekend. And maybe most disturbing of all is her clear indifference to her own disfiguration.

I think again of the whiter-than-white Q-tip. No, I regret nothing. I am what I want to be.

"What are you expecting of me?"

My question quavers. Where has the Voice gone? Where have the capital letters gone?

"What I'm expecting," says Louise, "has nothing to do with you. With anyone. But there's no one apart from you I feel like telling about it."

Louise throws her cig butt onto the floor and stamps on it.

"I've rubbed up against lots of bodies, you know, but I've never . . . well, I'm a virgin."

She smiles. Crooked teeth, but still white, far too white. I don't understand. I don't want to understand. I think of the Q-tip. I don't want to listen to what's coming, no, I don't want to, but it's me I hear saying:

"You Are Going to Give Birth."

Iris

I go into the cafeteria. I don't take a tray—rules are for visible people. I push in ahead of everyone, ahead of the prince. On today's menu: tabbouleh, eggs, yogurt, spinach, tomato sauce, and chicken thighs. I take a bit of everything (except spinach) with fingers I haven't washed for days. I give them a quick wipe on Vanessa's scarf; she'll get mad about it later, too late, when the sauce will have really crusted up. I swipe all the sugar sachets, not for me, just for the sake of it. I steal a packet of chips in one pocket, for me this time, for this evening, for my hideout, when the cafeteria will be empty and I'll feel peckish. Don't think about the night, not so soon, not yet.

I leave just as I arrived. Invisible, sure, but not inviolable. Must stop off at the infirmary, while it's open, to stock up on tampons. Here, everything, or nearly everything, is locked up after six, and I can't pass through doors.

I pass my sister in the corridor, flanked by her friends. Her laughter makes me puke. I cracked once. I grabbed her hand, the hand that ditched me, Here, from the very first day, and I screamed, screamed, screamed until I was split in two. Ingrid didn't flinch. Same with Mom. Every time Mom's car, with my half-brothers wriggling gleefully inside, stops outside the school to drop off or pick up my sister, and I call out, and implore, and implode, unable to get through this beastly gate, she doesn't flinch. I can see her clearly, her profile, her stray strand of hair, her limp hands on the steering wheel, and she, who more than anyone in the world should see me back—I did squat in her belly for nine months after all—she can't fucking see me at all. Maybe because she never did really look at me.

Fine. I'm nothing anymore to my family; my family's nothing anymore to me. Here is now my home. My trap.

Lessons have begun again for the afternoon. I go from class to class, I jostle students who don't react, steal from their bags, and the teachers', too, anything that might help me survive the night to come. My pilfering goes less unnoticed than I do. On Tuesday, the principal gathered the whole school under the shelter, when it was freezing, and waffled on and on for an hour about "respecting other people's property." I stole his watch, for a laugh, except it didn't make him laugh one bit when he noticed, and me not that much, either. So, for now, I'm sticking to my daily pickings. Apart from music, togs, and cigs, I don't scavenge much. But I do need something to send me to sleep.

During the next recess, I go to the library to find a really tedious book. It sometimes works, not always, depends on whether I let myself be lured by the words rather than by sleep. I wonder if the girl who doesn't pluck between her eyebrows will be there, at the library. I've sat two or three times beside her. She reads, writes, reads again, and sometimes, without warning, she looks up and straight at me, and her eyes aren't like other eyes, they're not short-sighted eyes, and every time I think that's it, here we go, the spell is lifted, but then she returns to her reading and I'm invisible once more.

I open the library door. The girl's not there. Instead, I'm dropped right in the middle of a meeting of the Top-Secret

Club: spotty teens hiding under a table, all in a huddle. There's intense whispering, la-di-da language, and wanting to seem important while crunching candies. They talk of "distortion" and "chmoll" ("chimoil"? "shmoyle"?).

I grab a random book and bounce. I never linger in the library, it's too much like Daddy's place, before he decided to quietly die on us, and Mom moved us into the stepfather's place. No library at the stepfather's place. No words.

I'm dropping from not enough sleep. I could head for my hideout, the store near the tech lab, where the soldering irons, reels of wire, and printed circuits are kept—what's left of them, at least, seeing as the latch is busted. I could, yes, except, in fact, I can't. As long as there's just one lesson going on in this school, even optional subjects, even dead languages, I'll be there. So what if the others can't see me anymore, I need to see the others, because as soon as I'm alone Here, in the cold shadows of the evening, and I find myself in front of a mirror, a pane of glass, a puddle that refuses to reflect me, it's as if I'm losing myself, and indeed, I am losing myself a little every night, since I've reached the point of not being afraid anymore. Being scared stiff is all I've got left.

It's the walls. It's always been them. They're trying to swallow me up. I tried climbing over them in the schoolyard and the sports grounds, even bleeding from the barbed wire, and the same thing happened as with the gate: I can't get beyond them, though I can see the street. Something is blocking me. All I do is tumble backwards every time.

I even tried approaching the miracle woman, in Room 1, with her sparrow feather around her neck, but she miracled fuck all, and, in any case, I think she's stopped now.

And there it goes.

The bell.

The very last one.

Today's Friday, and if there's one thing worse than the night Here, it's the weekend. I watch students and teachers rushing to get out with the same impatience. I walk against the flow for the physical pleasure of feeling shoulders knocking mine. My wandering takes me outside the only classroom I never enter, never pinch a thing from; it's a matter of principle.

Émile's class.

He's there. Alone. Standing in the middle of the empty desks. Naked. The boys (or girls?) have stuck his own briefs over his head and scrawled on them in black marker: "pervert." He's so thin, his ribs catch the twilight.

I quickly look away. I can see anything, watch anything, except that. Émile's loneliness makes me feel even more lonely.

I'm about to scoot when he begins to move. He doesn't take the briefs off, he bangs into chairs, he's looking for something. The window. I watch him out of the corner of my eye, through the gap in the door, without crossing the threshold of his class, as if that only half-counted. He stays there, stuck like a stake, in front of the window, with his bottom bare. He must be freezing, but he seems to be waiting. Waiting for what?

Number Three: "Will jump? Won't jump?"

I take a proper look this time. There's another student in the classroom I hadn't spotted until now. A weirdo. He's leaning on the radiator at the back and eyeing Émile with curiosity. Is he responsible for the briefs stunt?

"Bastard."

My voice is all croaky. The guy drops Émile. He looks at

me from the radiator. I look at him from the door. Our eyes collide like meteorites.

Number Three: "You can see me?"

"You can see me, too?"

So staggered am I that I almost forget Émile, totally lost there, in front of his window. He, at any rate, can't see us, can't hear us.

I walk right in. The guy studies me carefully as I approach. It feels strange to me. Enjoyably strange. As if I existed once more. But watch out: I might have broken a ton of rules since being invisible, but that one, never: I will not blub.

Number Three: "So, it's you, the disappearance."

I should be delighted that there's at least someone who's noticed my absence, but, dunno, the way he says it makes me feel uncomfortable. As if it was me, but it could just have well been anyone.

"My name's Iris. And yours?"

He says nothing. Seems to be considering the question very seriously. He has slightly twisted lips, with the scar typical of those born with a harelip.

Number Three: "A disappearance, too. The one from last year. It's stupid, but I've since forgotten my name."

He looks me over again, even more closely. And with amusement.

Number Three: "You should have a wash."

I rub my fingers, covered in dried sauce, on my jeans.

Émile hasn't moved. He's gazing at the sky, a red expanse, ice-cold and cloudless, through the weave of his briefs. Or maybe he's gazing at the tarmac of the schoolyard down below, but I prefer to think it's the sky.

Number Three: "Won't jump. Not this time, anyhow."

Sure enough, Émile finally gets dressed again. Slowly. Puts his things away. Slowly. Leaves. Slowly.

I find myself alone with the guy, but less alone than before. Less alone than Émile. There was once, I believe—it's so long ago!—a time when he and I would share everything, marbles, candies, pens, balls, kisses. He already found jumping over elastics hard, Émile, so from a window . . . The guy's talking crap.

"How do we get out of here?"

Number Three: "We don't get out."

"So, what do we do?"

Number Three: "We watch."

"Watch what?"

The guy gives a twisted smile. Darkness falls on us.

Number Three: "The next end of the world."

113

Pierre

No more consultations.

That's what's written on the door of Room 1. The ink has run, due to the rain. I knock just in case. No reply. I've already trekked four times to the back of the school, and each time it's been total silence. And I'm not the only one. Yesterday, while hiding in the parking lot during recess, what a stream of students, and a few teachers, too, I saw braving the rain to try their luck with the guru. They all found no one in.

Even me, who everyone hits but no one talks to, yup, even me, I've heard plenty of stories. Bodies changed. Lives altered. Well, from what I've gathered, it was mainly skin, weight, and dick problems.

Not sure if she can help me, the guru, but, like, nothing ventured . . .

I return to the schoolyard, shoulders hunched, hood over my eyes. I really don't want to see what I know I'll see if I turn my head, even a little. Follows me everywhere, the bastard.

All the plebs hurry under the shelter. The guru must be somewhere in the crowd. She was a student like any other before, less than any other, even, seeing that no one actually knows which class she's in, including those in her class.

I look for her without knowing how I'll recognize her. I find her. Maybe because Vincent has sat himself right beside her on a bench and is gesticulating wildly at me. Precedes me, now, the bastard.

"Um. Hi."

The guru doesn't reply to me. She's stuffing her mouth with brioche like she's bulimic or something. It's wet and freezing cold, but she's wearing giant sunglasses, like some starlet wanting anonymity. But then, I can't see her feather. Apparently, it's the feather that does everything.

"Um. I've got a little favor to ask."

I could loosen my hood, but it quite suits me, this shrunken vision of the world. As long as I have the guru straight in front of me, I don't see Vincent beside her, Vincent and his fingers drumming patiently on his oboe case, Vincent and his intolerable elastic smile. He still sits as straight as ever. Motherfucker.

In the meantime, the guru, she's still eating her brioche and saying nothing.

"Um. If it's about money . . ."

I hand her a banknote, a biggie, fresh out of the parental wallet, the sort I usually reserve for my bullies. I don't hold myself straight like Vincent, me. I'm so hunched, I almost can't breathe anymore.

"Could do better."

That's what she blurts, the guru, her mouth still full. There's something disturbing behind her dark glasses. Maybe it's her hairless skin or something, but she looks like a doll. No, like a baby. A fat, sulky baby, yup, but a baby who smells really nice.

She adds, without really looking at me (hard to tell with the sunglasses):

"That's what teachers have said about me since elementary school. Could do better. I'd grind three times more than Louise. Could do better. In track, in class, in collage, in coloring, in sewing, in dictation. Louise: first. Me: could do better. And for once, the one time I do better, the one time I'm finally special at something, well, no, Louise, she does even more better. For me, the shit of mediocrity. For her, a miracle, the real deal."

I don't know what to say to her. So, I ask again:

"About that little favor, you okay with it? It's kinda urgent. Um. I have to rid myself of an undesirable."

Vincent bursts out laughing, at the other end of the bench. Motherfucker. I pull the drawstring of my hood to keep him in my blind spot. From time to time, I get whacked on the nape or the ass, always from behind, always stealthily, and I should be relieved that at least that hasn't changed, that I'm still the odd number, the jack of spades, the lousy kid, that Vincent's totally dead for every-one—except me—but no, it's not enough, it's no longer enough for me.

If the guru can't see Vincent either, well, that's a good start.

"Um. So, you okay with helping me?"

"Ask Louise."

"Um. Who's Louise?"

"The girl who's been even more Chosen than me. The favorite of It. The Immaculate Conception. Well, let them carry on together, me, I'm pulling out and I'm just going to carry on could-do-bettering."

The bell. End of recess. Back to lessons. But personally, I don't fancy going back to anything at all.

"Go on, pleeease. Get rid of him for me, the wretch. I'll pay you whatever you want."

The guru stands up from the bench, almost seems to float up, a weightless baby, like she weighed nothing anymore, despite all the brioche she's guzzled, and I'm hit by a scent of flowers, of cut grass, of early summer that, yup, has a blissful effect on me. She's so close to me, the guru, that I can make out her eyes behind the sunglasses, eyes without eyebrows and without eyelashes.

"Let The Fratricide Be Haunted."

Fuck, what the hell was that voice? The guru gulps with distaste, then downs a soda in one, as if wanting to quickly swallow back those last words.

"The worst thing," she goes to me, in a normal voice this time, "is that however much I eat, however much I drink, nothing comes back out."

The guru is far away by the time I get my breath back. I, too, move away. From the bench, from Vincent, from his smile. I move away and I run, I run like an idiot, I don't return to the classroom with the others because I know, yup, I know he'll follow me there, wherever I go, in the corridors, the schoolyard, the corners, he follows me everywhere Here, from the first to the last bell, he follows me, without a word, he follows me, and the more I avoid him, the more he follows me.

I don't want to. Don't want to look at him properly. Don't want to see what I've done to him, since pushing him in the toilets from hell; a motherfucker of a ghost.

There's a gap in the wall, behind the sports ground, hidden by a fig tree. I climb, I cut class, I escape. On the pavement, in the rain, I run some more. I jump on the first bus to go past, I hide under my hood, I've got rain in my eyes, in my nose, but it's not that that's drowning me. I get off at a random stop, a wasteland, some public-housing projects, I don't know where I am and I don't care, as long as it's not Here.

I'm suffocating. I throw back my hood, and my head, and

my shoulders, and my back, I drink all the water from the sky. A little of my own water, too.

I turn around. Vincent is there, case in hand; he smiles. I'm not even that surprised. Just tired of running away from him, running away from me, from myself.

"What do you want from me?"

The smile widens. Vincent opens his case. The instrument is there, in its place, in separate pieces. Is there such a thing as an oboe's ghost?

"I don't get it."

Vincent looks at his oboe, and then at me, then at his oboe, then at me, until I do get it.

"Motherfucker."

I'm the odd number, the jack of spades, the lousy kid, but it's really me who's the motherfucker.

Guy

One length of the pool. And another. And go on, one more. I swim the crawl like a pro. Sofie's right (she's always right, Sofie, so much so that it's damned irritating): I love the swimming pool. On land, I drag myself around, weighed down by my bones. In the water, I rediscover something forgotten, something unignorable, a little something of who I was before turning into a clumsy oaf.

Whistle.

I push my goggles up onto my forehead. I grab the ladder, I come out of the pool, I'm dripping all over. Back to being ridiculous.

"Catch."

Ariane chucks me a towel. Not mine, the towel, but I dry myself.

"You're a great swimmer."

I try not to ogle Ariane's costume, even though she doesn't hold back from ogling my trunks; which she never did *before*. A drop of water hangs from her lip. You can smell the chlorine.

"Did it go okay, the essay?" she goes to me.

"Kinda, yeah."

Kinda too well, even. When my parents saw my grade, I earned myself a double dose of dessert at dinner. I even caught them, through the kitchen door, on my way to the bathroom at three in the morning, quietly going back over my whole essay. And stopping in the middle of a particularly brilliant sentence to clasp hands on the table in silence.

I instantly lost the need to piss.

Ariane clicks her tongue. The ex-lousy kid then turns tail, which is soaking wet, so I get that the towel was hers.

"I'll lend you my Bottom again anytime you like. Natural science. History. Trigonometry. She manages in almost every subject. You only need to ask, just treat yourself!"

Ariane is up close to me when she adds:

"You know the class opposite ours? They got tickets for some concerts. I'm sure they'd slip you some for free."

I say "yeah" to Arianne, but it's the prince I've got my eye on. He's sitting up in the gallery, fully dressed from head to toe, never seen in trunks, the prince. It's more him that's looking at me, with hands crossed in front of that face no one's allowed to get their fill of. Would Ariane ask him for free tickets, too?

Under the showers, all the Tops of the class pat me on the shoulder.

"Come to my place and we can play."

"So, that porn I gave you, did you like it?"

"Tomorrow we're cutting, come to the movies with us."

I say "yeah" to each of them. I make out that I'm cool with it all, but inside I'm totally buzzing. They never suggested doing anything with me *before*. I could almost cry— only almost, hey, there's a limit that even I, who they've all been flattering, yes, and fawning over for days now, even I can't go beyond, not that particular limit.

On the bus, I'm tossed a beer that I knock back with the rest of them. I come out with some pretty shit jokes. They all laugh, except the prince. With the back seat all to himself, and head deep in hood, he watches me.

We arrive at school in perfect time for the cafeteria. Even kids from other classes are saying "hi" to me and letting me go ahead of them. At the Tops' table, I get the best seat, a chair with no gum, spit, or sauce on it, a chair that doesn't wobble, doesn't jut out—didn't even know there were any of them left. And when I'd finished mine, they all offered me their fries.

"What have you decided?" Sofie asks.

I just sprawled out beside her, belly bursting, and she's already going on about it. Sunny today. A real warming sun, dandelions sprouting through cracks in the tarmac, like a false start to spring. Sofie has unpacked all her stuff outside, on the steps between the schoolyard and the parking lot, with a newspaper spread out on one step, a real grown-up one with baffling graphics, no horoscope, no run-over dogs, and in the margins of her newspaper, Sofie, like on all her books and photocopies, Sofie has gone and scrawled tons of notes. Or rather, tons of questions. She's forever asking herself questions, Sofie, questions about absolutely everything. Stupid questions like "What have you decided?", which she's gone and asked me every day since the prince offered me his deal.

Talking of the prince, he's there. In the parking lot, under his hood, sitting on top of the principal's car, holding a joint. He's watching me.

"I told him I'd think about it. Well, I'm thinking."

I don't speak loudly, even though the prince is too far away to hear.

Sofie underlines a word in her newspaper, and adds a big . . . what's it called again? A question mark.

"He'll end up deciding for you. In fact, he already has."

She glances at the rings glinting on my fingers. Usually, at the collection, I just get peanuts. This time, I was spoilt.

And when I wanted to pay Sofie's share, like I've done every month since the beginning of the year, all the Tops refused and paid out of their own pockets (well, their Bottoms' pockets), which made Sofie sigh.

"I'd be crazy not to accept. Being prince instead of the prince . . . a win-win for me."

Sofie says yes, not yes to me, though, yes to something else she suddenly thinks of. She's spotted him, too, the prince, over there, on the principal's car.

"And him?"

"What about him?"

"By swapping his position for yours. What does he himself gain?"

She's depressing me now, Sofie, with her questions.

"How the hell do I know. Not my problem."

I'm good at that: sweeping stuff away. It's like my parents, clasping hands over that essay I didn't write a word of. Swept away. Like Sofie, in the library, where she told me what she should never have told me. Swept away. And that way she has now of staring at my pool-mussed hair and cap-marked forehead, nothing like Ariane ogling my trunks, because Sofie's eyes see me, really see the real me, and because they scare me a little, too. Swept away. And all that I've never asked Sofie, why she never comes to sports classes, why she changed school, what her life's like beyond the gate. Swept away.

Under the carpet goes pathos. I keep only what suits me.

"Right," goes Sofie. "And after?"

"What about after?"

"You accept to take the prince's place. And after that? The teachers up your grades, the others overpay you, your diploma just falls into your lap. And after that? After Here, what will you do? Who will you be?"

I'm up on my feet. Really pissed, that's it.

"You know what? I've decided. I'm accepting. And you know what? I'm accepting because of you. You told me you'd teach me to listen. I listened, and you know what? It taught me nothing. I'm not you, and you know what? I don't want to be you. If taking the prince's place means I don't have to put up with all your nonsense, well, you know what? That suits me just fine."

I leave Sofie standing there and storm off. Not to the parking lot, not to the prince, no, in the opposite direction, need to be alone, I hug the walls to avoid the ass-kissers, don't even know where I'm going, pace around and around the schoolyard, even when the bell rings, I keep going to calm myself down, and so what if I'm late for class, I'm the next prince, after all, so quit the crap. Everything's spinning around the schoolyard with me: my parents' hands, the drop of water on Ariane's lip, the pats on my shoulders, Sofie's question marks, the prince watching.

Why's it jangled my nerves like this?

I climb the stairs up to the fourth floor.

I take a quick look at the board in the corridor. No change there for now. My name's written in chalk above Sofie's, and still, that "equals" sign there, between us.

I go into the classroom. The teacher has already started his lesson, indicates to me to sit down, far too politely. All eyes are on me. The eyes of the Tops, the eyes of the Bottoms. In the middle of the room, the prince's desk is free, waiting just for me, and, like, I know that the second I sit my ass down there, instead of my name on the board in the corridor, well, it'll be the prince's, his real name before he became prince.

He's sitting on my chair. Beside Sofie.

He's not watching me anymore; it's towards her that his hood is turned; and I finally get what he gains from this.

And Sofie, fuck it, Sofie's bawling. Without hiding it, without blowing her nose, in front of the whole class, staring wide-eyed, eyebrow fiercely frowning, nose red and swollen, she's bawling. And it's not because of the prince that Sofie's bawling her eyes out, but because of me, of my words, of my shit.

I go and stand in front of the prince. In front of my place. I pull off all my rings, and almost my fingers with them.

"I refuse."

The prince's hood doesn't move, a weighty silence, and then his hand goes up, so weighty that silence, and then he snaps his fingers. Silence over. Everyone boos me, and whistles at me, and insults me, the teacher protests, Sofie suddenly stands up, not crying anymore (whew), I think she's speaking to me, but I can't hear a thing anyhow, there's shouting from all directions, even the Bottoms are hollering, and when yelling isn't enough anymore, the blows follow.

The Substitute Teacher

The rasp of markers on paper. I like that noise. It means they've got stuff to write. It'll be less great this weekend, when their work will have to be graded. Grades aren't really my thing, or really the students' thing, but they're the minister's thing, and the principal's thing, and the parents' thing. So that's that.

I observe the class. Not *my* class, *the* class. When you're a substitute, nothing ever really belongs to you, and that suits me fine. I'm a transitional being, a little hyphen.

So, I observe. There are two at the back not writing anymore. Madeleine and Louise. They always complete everything before the others, as if racing against the clock, in a hurry to finish. Sitting side by side; I can almost see the wall between them. An old wall. Older, at any rate, than Madeleine's bilious attack. Since giving up her obscure rituals and quest for the absolute at the other end of the building, she's been sulking. Constantly. The queen of miracles brought back down to earth and anonymity. Hard not to notice her, though, Madeleine. I didn't know her before—she was already spending recesses in her cellar when I was posted Here—but you'd think she was undergoing chemo.

I observe Louise, too. She crosses her arms over her work, which I'm sure is excellent, but there's something stirring under her smoothness. I can almost see something hidden inside her. Something secretly contained, but that, sooner or later, will want to come out. What is it?

"Louise."

I waited for the test to be over and the others to bolt (the weekend rush) to keep her back.

"Miss."

"Your homework impressed me. Would you be happy to read it in front of the class, on Monday?"

Louise considers it.

"I authorize you to read it for me."

Madeleine is lingering by the door. Her eyes are inscrutable, but her feet, squeezed tight to together, don't lie. The feet never lie; maybe that's why I don't like them. I hope I haven't aggravated anything.

Bring on tonight's phone call.

I collect all the tests, lock up the class, walk down the stairs. Between the second and first floors, some brats are knocking about another brat, the odd one in the crew. They're from the missing boy's class. I send them packing. The odd one doesn't thank me; his eyes are half-hidden by his bangs; he's excessively hunched up. Just for one moment, I almost see someone right up close to him in the stairs. Someone holding a case? I hope it's not who I think it is.

Bring on that phone call.

I walk slowly. Everyone has swiftly cleared the building. The staff room is empty, or almost. Anatole is—yet again—yelling at his teen son.

"You really take me for a fool. Every Thursday, for god's sake. How many times do I have to punish you? Cutting the same class every week. The same class. Every week. What the hell's he going to think, my colleague? What the hell are they going to think, all my colleagues? And your mother? What the hell's she going to think, your mother?"

Number One: "All this goes far beyond our personal interests, Dad. Punish me and let's not mention it anymore."

Anatole's shoulders slump. It's been beyond him from the start. He must be the only person Here who doesn't know of the existence of the Top-Secret Club. Quite a good club, what's more. If they've already understood about Thursday-2:28, these young things, they're doing well.

Anatole suddenly notices me, standing by my locker. Awkward. He pushes the teen out of the staff room, less roughly than he'd have liked to (that, too, I almost see).

"Apologies . . . Thérèse, isn't it? A difficult day."

He empties what's left in the coffeepot into a beaker. Hesitates. Offers it to me. Very classy. I'm dying to go home, to lift the receiver, to hear the voice, but I never turn down coffee.

And Anatole needs to let off steam.

"A great lump of a boy almost got lynched during my lesson. He ended up in the infirmary. The prince's class. What a nightmare, that class."

There's fear in his words. And distress. And regret. I gaze at his pigeon-toed feet.

He smiles, pityingly.

"I shouldn't tell you that. Not you. You were a student at this establishment. I was told that . . . anyhow, it can't have been a bed of roses, either. But really, they're appalling this year. Even my own kids . . . they took things so seriously before. And now, one damned idiocy after another. What if they become like them? Lynchers. Liars. Abusers. Torturers, the lot of them, even the victims! It's going from bad to worse."

"No," I respond.

"No?"

He's increasingly lost, Anatole. I almost regret having knocked back the last of the coffee.

I smile.

"It's not going from bad to worse. It's cyclical. You, too, were like them, either at this Here, or another. You've forgotten, that's all."

No more fear in Anatole, boom, gone. Instead, indignation. He stomps out. I've never been good at making friends, especially Here. It reminds me of my own Thursday-2:28.

I empty my locker, leave my key. Bring on the phone.

"Sorry."

A woman stops me in the corridor, just as I'm leaving. A student's mom. Despite what she's just said, she doesn't look the sort to apologize.

"We need to talk about my daughter."

"Your daughter?"

"Ingrid."

She hands me a grade book. Ah, yes, I recognize the photo. Final year Here, I take her class on Tuesday. Decent grades, plenty of friends, girls and boys. A strong personality, Ingrid, but hardly what we'd call a problem student.

"What's the concern?"

"That's for you to tell me," the mom answers, annoyed.

I really don't know how to respond to that. And over there, in the apartment, my phone will soon be ringing.

"Maybe consult her class's regular teacher?"

But it's me the mom follows out to the schoolyard, her feet sticking close to mine. More than furious, she looks tired. Extremely tired.

"I'm in a hurry, too. They're waiting for me in the car. All of them."

Aha. A lack of conviction in those last three words. I

shouldn't, but never mind, the phone will wait. Let's call it intuition.

"What do you think I should have said to you?"

She sits on a schoolyard bench, rummages in her bag; hunting for her keys, I think. Her movements are uncoordinated.

"I can clearly sense something's wrong."

"Something's wrong with Ingrid?"

"No. Well, yes. I really don't know, myself. It can't be explained. It's not the same as it was."

She wipes a hand over her mouth, a mouth that doesn't smile much. And going by her hoarse voice, a mouth that doesn't talk much, either.

"Something's wrong. My daughter . . . something's wrong."

Maybe due to the memories, of my own Thursday-2:28, my intuition is confirmed. An awful intuition.

I sit down beside her on the bench, where she's spread out all her things. I look more carefully at Ingrid's grade book, in the middle of crumpled tissues, mini-bottles of grenadine, and scattered loyalty discount cards.

"Are we actually talking about your daughter? About that daughter?"

"Who else?"

The mom shuddered. I understood.

She pushes up the shoulder strap of her bag, then a strand of hair that's escaped from her clasp, then her sleeve to uncover the watch on her wrist.

"I must go. They're waiting for me in the car. All of them."

Again, that uncertainty when saying *all of them*.

"I'll make an appointment with the regular teacher."

She leaves. And now here I am, alone on the bench, in this schoolyard that emptied like water from a bath. Alone? Really? I frown, screw up my eyes. I neither see, nor almost see anything around me, but I can't stop thinking about that mom. About her daughter. About that other girl who, I'm sure now, isn't Ingrid.

I stand up. I mustn't get involved, mustn't interfere; each to their own story, mine is over. I'd like my feet to carry me away, far from Here, but they don't budge. My memory's in overdrive, recollections are choking me.

It could be me. It has already been me.

I speak out loud:

"Right. I can't see you, but I think you can see me. If you are there, then listen carefully, because I won't repeat it. Telling it to you once, that's already cheating. Are you listening? Those who disappear are often excellent observers. But—listen carefully now—it's enough for one thing, just one thing not to have been seen. Really seen. One thing that will have to be looked at. That's it."

My feet finally consent to leave. I rush to the gate, perhaps afraid of not being able to get through it anymore. Once in the street, I feel stupid. And yet I did know it, that my own story was over.

Bring on the phone.

Third Term

The Top-Secret Club

Number Two: "Stinks like hell here, fuck's sake."

Number One: "Well, we are in the basement. The whole school's dirty water passes through here. Not to mention all the inappropriate things our classmates throw down the toilets. Bring the flashlight closer, I need to check something."

Number Two: "Where are you? Yo, there you are."

Number One: ". . ."

Number Two: ". . ."

Number One: ". . ."

Number Two: "And all those quitters, fuck's sake. 'We've got better things to do, blah blah blah . . . Not enough results, blah blah blah . . . It only lands us in the shit, blah blah blah . . .' No kidding, hey, it's classy, our club."

Number One: "Two is always more than one. Right. According to the floor plan, we should take the next tunnel on the left."

Number Two: "And you?"

Number One: "What about me?"

Number Two: "Well . . . aren't there times when you think . . . I dunno . . . that we got a bit worked up, y'know? That all that stuff about the *intramural distortion of the field of reality*, y'know, well, it's all bullshit? That basically, there's never been an end of the world to stop?"

Number One: "Never."

Number Two: "Okay."

Number One: ". . ."

Number Two: ". . ."

Number One: "And you?"

Number Two: "Me, well, dunno. I won't let you down. I'll never let you down. My shoes are ruined, fuck's sake."

Number One: ". . ."

Number Two: ". . ."

Number One: ". . ."

Number Two: "You don't get the feeling we're being followed?"

Number One: "Did you hear someone?"

Number Two: "No."

Number One: "Did you see something?"

Number Two: "No, no. It's just . . . as if . . . dunno."

Number One: ". . ."

Number Two: ". . ."

Number One: "Right. We're there. We should be there, at any rate, if the floor plan is accurate. Move the flashlight closer, can't see a thing."

Number Two: "That's mainly because there's nothing to see. Walls. Pipes. Piss. More pipes. Where d'you get it from, your floor plan?"

Number One: "The school archives. I picked a few locks. Time by your watch?"

Number Two: "2:21."

Number One: "Feel like laughing?"

Number Two "Not really."

Number One: "Me neither. It might still be a bit early. Let's wait."

Number Two: ". . ."

Number One: ". . ."

Number Two: "2:25."

Number One: ". . ."

Number Two: ". . ."

Number One: ". . ."

Number Two: "There. 2:28. And we're definitely not laughing."

Number One: "We're in the right place at the right time. It's necessarily, mathematically through here that the schmoil arrives before flowing into the gutter outside. We really are very close, we should have felt its effects. Aha."

Number Two: "What?"

Number One: "Look at the floor plan. These lines, they're the main pipes. We're at this location. You see that line, there, which leads directly to Here, very clearly? Do you see where it comes from?"

Number Two: "From some distance. Isn't that the sports grounds, over there?"

Number One: "Almost. The toilets from hell."

Number Two. "Fuck's sake. You mean the schmoil, it comes to us from there?"

Number One: "Help me."

Number Two: "To do what?"

Number One: "There's a valve here. Help me turn it."

Number Two: "That huge fucking thing? It's all rusty. We'll catch that teta whatsit."

Number One: "No great advances are achieved without small sacrifices."

Number Two: ". . ."

Number One: ". . ."

Number Two: "Right, we've reached the max now, can't turn any more. What's this going to do?"

Number One: "No idea. Maybe nothing. Maybe everything."

Number Two: "And now?"

Number One: "Now we go back up. We go back up and we wait. We wait and we observe."

Number Two: "Fuck's sake."

Iris

Number Three: "They're such wackos."

I watch the two shadows moving off and disappearing down the tunnel, but Thingy and me, we're even more shadowy.

"The wackos did have a flashlight and a floor plan."

The darkness in the basement clings to us. A putrid darkness. I want to get back up to the surface; I want some air, and some light, and some concrete; I want a hand to hold. Thingy always keeps his hands in his pockets.

Number Three: "Don't need crap like that to see. Just eyes. So use yours. And shut up."

Always the same old song. I get to hear it every night, when he forces me to switch the light off in our hideout, every weekend, when he locks me in the changing-room cupboards—use your eyes!—and me screaming, not out of blind panic, no, out of principle, because, when I can't see any of me anymore, my voice is the last proof of my existence Here.

This time, I keep quiet. I open my eyes wide because we came down to the basement on purpose, because Thingy has trained me for it, even if he hasn't yet told me why. I'm not sure I like him, but I trust him. He's been invisible for a long time.

One thing that will have to be looked at, right?

So, I look. I look at the dark. And behind it, I look at

even more darkness. I look at the filthy smells. I look at the wet noises. I look, and I keep quiet, and, finally, I see. I see Thingy beside me. I see the scar on his lip, the ironic smirk. I even see his hands inside his pockets, I see the melted, bumpy skin of his fingers, the missing nails that never grew back, I see the chemical set, the toxic mix, the stupid accident. I see his past?

I see his eyes that see my eyes.

Number Three: "That's fine. You're ready."

"For what?"

Number Three: "For the future."

I follow him. One tunnel after another, tons of gloom. We walk for a long time. All this emptiness under the school, all this nothingness . . . I find it strangely consoling.

Number Three: "We're there."

A dead end. At the deepest and furthest part of the school. I don't get it. I screw up my eyes. No, not like that. Just see. I relax all the muscles of my face, my body. Facing the wall, I leave myself behind.

Words leap out, in giant fluorescent graffiti.

Disappearance.

Murder.

Revolution.

Birth.

The same words, tagged and retagged, extending beyond the real boundaries of the wall.

Disappearance. Murder. Revolution. Birth. Disappearance. Murder. Revolution. Birth. Disappearance. Murder. Revolution. Birth. Disappearance. Murder. Revolution. Birth. Disappearance. Murder. Revolution. Birth.

And then I get it.

"It's a loop. A wretched loop."

Number Three: "Disappearance and murder, they've happened. Revolution and birth, they're coming. If everything keeps going, the cycle will be complete before the summer vacation. It's not every year there's a fucking clear round."

He lights a cigarette—homestyle: Thingy rolls his with muck filched from the chemistry lab, which goes off with a fart in his face half the time. The lighter creates a brief bubble of brightness between us.

"And after that?" I ask. "If the four predictions are fulfilled this year? What happens then?"

Number Three: "An end of the world. And then, snap, another cycle starts off. Until the next end of the world. Etcetera, etcetera."

"Have you seen a lot of them, yourself, these ends of the world?"

Number Three: "None. But I know someone who experienced one. Not a pretty sight, apparently."

I've got the jitters. *Disappearance.* I touch the tag in front of me. It's more fluo than the rest, fresher. Is that all I am? Thirteen letters among thousands of others on a moldy old wall in the basement? A role from a script written long ago? How many have there been before me, before Thingy, of these disappearances? How many will there be after? How many worlds ended Here before starting again? And why am I suddenly thinking of Émile, of his stripped ass, of that way he's had, since then, of hanging around windows, whenever I catch sight of him?

One thing that will have to be looked at.

"That someone, who is it?"

Number Three: "Another person who disappeared. Way before me. Théophile."

"The upside-down student? He doesn't exist. I've never seen him."

Number Three: "Because he doesn't want to be seen. But Théophile, he sees everything."

"Fine. If he exists, I must meet him."

Number Three: "What for? He's a pain in the ass."

"All this has to stop."

He sniggers. He never laughs, Thingy, always sniggers.

Number Three: "If you still hope, then you're way dumber than you look."

His cigarette flickers in the dark when he takes a drag. No, I don't like him, and sometimes we can barely stand each other. Often, during the week, we split up for hours, each lurking in their little corner of the schoolyard, and whatever we swipe, whether food, beer, or knickknacks, we don't share. But when the whole school clears off, we return to each other. I need his gaze just like he needs mine.

"The other day, my mother came Here . . ."

Number Three: "About your sister. About Ingrid."

"About me. We don't disappear completely. We leave a trace. And what that teacher said afterwards . . ."

Number Three: "To nobody."

"To me. *One thing that hasn't been really seen. One thing that will have to be looked at.* That's what I'm going to do. You were saying that Théophile sees everything, right? Get us a meeting."

The cigarette butt falls, a red streak in the darkness.

Number Three: "You do my head in. I showed you the future, Iris, isn't that enough for you? What more do you want?"

"To reappear."

Pierre

The conservatoire next door. First time I've set foot in it.
Lawn everywhere outside, parquet everywhere inside. Music
in every corner. Chords on keyboards, sour notes from a clarinet, strings here, brasses there, singing that rises and then
suddenly breaks off: a strangely beautiful racket.

I'm all clammy. My case slides in my hand. I go up some
stairs; parquet, too, on the stairs. It's like my folks' house. I
feel out of place.

In front of me, Vincent leads the way. Not a crease in his
trousers, nape shaved ruler-straight, supple and thick, he's
not walking anymore, no: he's swimming. His very own,
real Here.

He indicates a door to me, with a smile. I walk in.

Heads swivel in my direction. Very young ones and less
young ones; none of my age. Not that many heads, around
a dozen, but already too many for me. I prefer backs. The
teacher's not here yet. I go straight to the back to sit down.
They all turn in my direction without a word, seeming to
wonder, who the hell is this guy? All togged up like Vincent,
they are.

It looks like a class, without quite being one. There are
staves already drawn on the board, a piano instead of the
teacher's desk, a smell of polished wood, and crucially, crucially, just a single desk per student. No sharing. So, no odd
one.

This place is nothing like another Here. It's an *elsewhere*. I'm just so totally out of place.

Vincent smiles at me, backlit by a window. The sun makes everything in the room glow—the varnished wood, the piano keys, the metal music stands—except him.

"Apologies, I'm late."

A little dude closes the door behind him, opens all the windows, loosens his bow tie (a bow tie, seriously,) and hands out sheets of paper. A teacher who apologizes? That's a first, too.

He stops a bit short on seeing me, then seems to remember.

"Pierre, isn't it? Do you have a grasp of musical notation?"

I garble something, and even I don't know what I'm trying to say. Vincent smiles even more—asshole.

The little dude gives me some sheet music. A whiff of photocopier. Apart from that, nothing looks familiar on this piece of paper. Seems like a different language.

"You're joining us a bit late. I can't promise to get you aboard the moving train, but still, your parents have paid for it."

Yup. They looked vaguely surprised when I asked them to enroll me at the conservatoire. Usually, it's a games console or some shoes. That'll teach me to shove people into pits, won't it.

"You won't be needing that," says the little dude, seeing me open my case. "In this class, we work on sightreading, not instrument playing. Watch and listen. Join in if you like."

The little dude chatters and tinkles away on the piano at the same time. Doesn't even look at his fingers on the keyboard. He doesn't seem the least bit little to me anymore. Eraser-tipped pencils drum on desks. Voices are raised.

Quarter note-half note-triplet-eighth note-whole note-quarter note dotted-do-mi flat-la-sharp-treble clef-bass clef-alto clef.

I watch. I listen. I don't join in. I don't understand a thing.

Vincent smiles; not at me, to himself. He taps the sole of his shoe soundlessly, to the beat of the metronome.

No bell at the conservatoire. Just the little dude giving us a "See you next week!" and a whole load of exercises to plow through at home. As if I didn't have enough homework, c'mon.

"There. I came. I tried. It's not my thing. You're going to leave me alone now, okay?"

I stretch out on the lawn; Vincent sits beside me, upright, his case on his thighs. The sound of a brass band filters out through the windows. The sun's already clearing off, and I'm tempted to do the same. I've got another class in fifteen minutes. A one-to-one lesson. The worst of the worst for an odd one.

"Fine," I say. "I'll go back in there one last time. One last time, d'you hear?"

Vincent looks pleased. The idiot.

He's playing the guide again, along the corridors of the conservatoire. Through half-opened doors, hands swirl over a harp, bows go up and down, shoulders broaden, necks swell, and all those butts on stools, those spines that have lengthened without chair-backs, it's all too upright for me; or I'm too twisted for it. No rules, just systems. It's like at those classical concerts: everything's calculated down to the last pube, including the applause.

The oboe room is empty. I hang about with Vincent. Increasingly gloomy. I don't dare switch on the light. Barely dare to be.

"Ah. The surprise student."

The teacher arrives three hours late. And she doesn't apologize. Her tiny eyes are buried behind three layers of kohl.

"Did you pay for it?"

"Um. Yes, Miss."

She opens my case, assembles my oboe. I feel dispossessed. Vincent smiles.

"You shouldn't have. A beginner rents. Buying, that's committing. You look like someone who's already regretting your decision."

The teacher spreads an array of reeds on a desk. Chooses one. Scrapes it. Tests it. Fixes it to the oboe.

"First lesson, you blow into it. Chin in. Lips pinched. Mouth pursed. Without puffing out the cheeks. Abdominal breathing. Wedge your thumb well under. Up higher, your elbows. And your back, there, that's not going to work, need to sort all that out, fast. But first blow."

I blow. Like I so often watched Vincent blow, in our cleaning store, after lessons, before the gate, ten minutes during which I'd lose myself through him. I blow. I empty my lungs, lungs I never knew were that full. Or that compressed. I blow. As if all this time I'd been holding my breath, years without breathing, an entire life without air. I blow. Something behind me straightens, my back aches. I revive my first yelp as a newborn. I stop blowing. I've grown ten centimeters.

The teacher's eyes have gotten bigger.

"That was . . . not too bad. Better than that, even. You've got quite some blow."

Vincent smiles. And me, though I don't want to, though I've no right to want to, I smile, too.

I'm the odd number, the jack of spades, the lousy kid, and the murderer of your student, Miss.

Guy

The seconds pass. Not the tick-tock kind, with hands, which always confuse me, no, not my watch. No: a good square face, digital display, big and bold.

I wait. The bell's gone. Allow time for them to trudge up to the fourth, jostle, greet, chat, flirt, gorge on candies and weed. For each Top to fleece each Bottom: biochemistry homework, crib sheets, and—for those not satisfied with the collection—allowance. In short, for all those little deals to be done before the teacher turns up.

They must be in their seats now. The prince, too.

My turn now.

I creep out from my corner of the corridor, between the emergency exit and the mop cupboard. I enter the class-room. Everyone suddenly goes quiet, then everyone goes back to talking, but louder than before. I lower my head. Wish I could bury it right inside me.

I scoot between the desks.

It's almost like before. The Tops beside their Bottoms. The prince, who's still prince, lording it alone in the middle, bothered by no one, served by everyone. And Sofie. Sofie in her seat, right-hand row, near the window, Sofie in the morning sun, jeans and sneakers under a dress, Sofie who looks at me, the only one to look at me, in fact, Sofie, with eyes so open that her lashes catch on her eyebrow.

She's done it again. She's put my chair back beside her.

145

Ta-dah. She gets everything, Sofie, except what she doesn't want to get.

I can feel her eyes on me while I re-re-retake my chair with my eyes cravenly fixed on my shoes, and drag it to the very back of the class, far behind the last desks, where no one will have to pretend not to see me anymore, except Sofie, who's craning her neck, who's blatantly eyeballing me, and silently asking me a question I don't have the answer to.

I sit down. Sit myself down? Take my seat? Fuck's sake, how should I be saying it?

Whatever, I wait. My back to the wall. When he arrives and sees me there, the teacher sighs but says nothing; they never say anything, the teachers, not in the presence of the prince. The teacher takes attendance. I raise half a hand when it's my name, and the whole class coughs at the same time. The teacher begins his lesson and, that's it, off to a new day with ass on my chair, nose on my watch, and Sofie's eyes on me.

Those of Ariane, of the others, they're far, far away.

My name's been crossed out. A big chalk line on the board in the corridor. Since the judgment, I'm no longer a Top, I'm not a Bottom, I've not become prince in place of the prince, I'm not even a sort of odd one. I'm nothing.

I haven't only lost face. I've lost everything else, too.

Makes a restful change. Pretending to be someone is damn tiring, so stop with your eyes, Sofie, pleeease.

At recesses, too, I wait in my seat. The prince stands up first, the others follow him without looking at him. And Sofie moves in the opposite direction.

She plonks herself in front of me.

"Why don't you come and sit back in your place?"

"I'm in it, my place."

"You're where you choose to be."

A few stragglers give Sofie dirty looks. She has always disturbed them, and her disturbing's getting worse and worse. My name's crossed out on the board: hers isn't. A Bottom without a Top, a Bottom who bawled in front of the whole class, a Bottom who the prince nearly paired up with, even if, since the judgment, he's not that interested in Sofie anymore; anyhow, a Bottom like that, who doesn't tick any little boxes, it looks pretty bad after a while. Does a Bottom like that even get collected from?

Not my problem anymore. No longer my Bottom; no longer her Top.

"You mustn't speak to me. I've been struck off."

"Guy."

So assured, her voice. So assured, her eyes. So altogether self-assured. Sofie's so present when she says my name, it's almost unbearable. Just makes me feel even more absent.

"You know where to find me."

And off she goes. To the library, as usual. Yeah, yeah, Sofie, I know where to find you. I just don't know where to look for myself anymore.

Finally, alone. An empty body in an empty classroom. A thing on a chair.

I take my grub out of my bag, just to fill myself up a bit. I unwrap the foil. Sliced bread, leftover ham, stinky cheese. I've quit going to the cafeteria; I scrounge from my parents' fridge. They don't say a thing anymore, my parents, since the judgment. Nothing when I say it's the stairs' fault I have black eyes. Nothing, either, when my grades tumbled back down. I think they've had it up to here, in fact.

I wait. A whole lotta seconds to go before the class gets back from the cafeteria.

"You're a disappointment."

I freeze, eyes fixed on my watch. The prince's voice. He's here, in the classroom, alone with me. He moves closer, with all his rings and other bling. I might not look directly at him, but hell, do I hear him. Our last tête-à-tête cost me big time.

From the corner of my eye, I think I see him grabbing Didier's chair, a Top in the back row. At first, I think he's going to smash it over my head. But instead, he sits (sits himself down? takes a seat? fuck's sake!) on it. Directly facing my chair.

It becomes hard not to look at him. I stare at his hands on his knees. He has seriously clear skin. Not a hair.

"In your opinion, dickhead. The deal I offered you. Why did I pick you, in particular?"

"You won't have Sofie."

It just burst out of me. Straight from the gut.

"No one can have her," I add.

Not even me. Especially not me. Sofie, she's . . . what's that word again? *Elusive*, and what's more, I'm sure I never knew that word before knowing Sofie; so maybe she did actually teach me to listen.

The prince laughs, a laugh that's not joking.

"I picked you because you're a loser. Because I'm bored out of my mind. Because I wanted to have some fun. Except there's nothing fun about you, you're just a loser."

Right then, it hits me like a flash:

"Your place. You never even considered passing it on to me."

The prince springs from the chair he's pinched from Didier and spits on it.

"My place is everywhere. Yours, you've lost it. So, stay at the back, dickhead. You're forbidden from sitting in your former place. If one day you're tempted to return to it, along-side your Bottom, I snap my fingers and you're dead. I make you bleed like you've never bled before. And that, yes, maybe that will be amusing."

I gaze at the gob of spit while the prince leaves. Dead, hey? I already am a bit, aren't I?

At home time, my father's there, in his taxi, as usual. My mother, too, in the passenger seat, but that's not usual. I quickly slam the car door. Off we go. I sit back from the windows so as not to be seen by Sofie, who I'm avoiding as much as I can, from the corridors to the sidewalks; and even more since the prince's little lunchtime chat. I'm not just hugging the walls, at this stage, I'm grazing myself on them.

"Where we going?"

Change of route. My father's not returning us to the fold.

"You'll see when we're there," goes my mother.

She's put on her earrings and Sunday-best dress for us. Shit. They've said nothing for too long, my parents. Major interrogation to come. Or worse: a visit to the guidance counselor. Again.

My father parks the car, we walk into a pizzeria, my mother hands me the menu.

"Choose whatever you like."

This stinks of a trap. I fall right into it, obviously. I order my fave pizza, extra large. Days of under-eating leftovers: I'm going to pay dearly for it, this pizza, one reproach per mouthful, but I don't leave a crust of it.

I wait.

The digits keep changing on my watch. My parents chew their lasagna in silence. No questions, just a little remark: well, makes a change from the frozen stuff. My father even splits his sides over some little joke. My mother bursts out

149

laughing—"you're daft"—and wipes some sauce off my chin with her napkin, having moistened it in her glass. When I was a kid, we'd go out to a restaurant like this whenever we were celebrating something. What the hell are we celebrating here? There's nothing to celebrate. Congratulations, *monsieur*, *madame*, your son's a loser. He's lost face and he'll never get it back. And same goes for his place.

I wait. I almost hope.

We go home. My father turns on the car radio, my mother turns up the volume. At the apartment, still no questions. They switch the TV on, and I'm even allowed to watch with them. They don't talk about my grades, my homework, my future. They don't talk. But when I mumble a half-hearted "good night," my mother makes a strange gesture, as if to keep me a little longer beside them, on the sofa.

Her hand falls back onto my father's, and they say to me: "See you tomorrow."

I go to bed. I think of all the criticism they didn't level at me. I think of my chair on which I'll wait for a future that'll never come. I think of the words Sofie once said to me, that she should never have said to me, and that she'll never say to me again. Words that I very nearly heard this evening. That I don't deserve. I think of all that and I do what I'll never do in front of anyone, cross my heart and hope to die. I sob.

Madeleine

"Take out your paints, have your color wheel handy. Flat brushes only. Today, you're each going to give birth to a town. What are they like, the buildings in a town? They're not the same. They layer each other, they vie with each other. Think about that. Silhouetting! Play with the dimensions, the textures, and especially, the colors. I want a bit of everything: primary, secondary, analogous, complementary, warm, cool. Inject a touch of spring, of twilight, of community into your town. And now let's hurry up, come on, come on, you'll be graded at the end of the hour."

In the class, plenty of noisy indignation, but not much hurrying. I furiously squeeze my tubes onto my palette: professional paint, paid for with Grandad's meager savings, which I waste with malicious satisfaction. I load my brush, then paint wobbly, crude, lumpy lines; I crunch up my paper and start over. Again. And again. And again.

I give birth to nothing.

Beside me, Louise's town is already spectacular. Her belly is, too. I'm definitely no expert on the subject, biology not being my fave, but it still seems to me that she's shooting ahead. But then, that's Louise for you. She was doing silent reading when I was struggling to decipher the alphabet, so nine months, come on, that's too long for her. The teacher smiles appreciatively over her shoulder—so slumped with boredom, Louise's shoulder!—and congratulates her: for her town, not her belly. No one mentions Louise's belly. Collective denial of a pregnancy.

Me, I don't deny. I renounce. I renounce Louise, I renounce her miniature miracle, growing in her saintly womb, and above all, I renounce the Voice. I threw the feather into the toilet. I've stopped answering the phone at home, and too bad if it makes Nan run from the garden. I get zeros in class participation. I don't talk about anything anymore with anyone, with no exception, including Louise, of course.

I'm totally determined to keep it shut until the end of the world. At least.

"You have ten minutes left. Don't forget about drying time."

I contemplate the cacophony of paint on my corner of the table. I've got it all over my fingers; the paper's still blank. I can't bear colors anymore. They're a distant thing, my rose windows. Fuck the rainbow.

It comes over me without warning.

I pilfer a pencil from Louise's case, and not any old one: her 2B. I push the tip over my paper, to the right, the left, down, up, anything but straight lines, I scratch with the lead, I wear it down, I clear away, through drawing, all that my body no longer secretes, excrement, menstrual blood, all I've stopped feeling on the surface and inside, the itchy, the painful, the delectable. The old body, flattened out!

"The bell will ring soon, clean your brushes and place your towns on my desk. But that's not the exercise asked for, Madeleine! What on earth is that?"

I'm asking myself the same question. I have to admit that I'm more baffled than anyone by what I've scrawled across the paper. It's hideously beautiful. Fabulously ugly.

The teacher takes my drawing.

"It's . . . It's . . ."

The teacher's face contorts. Her jaw tightens, her lips quiver, and a moist film forms over her bulging eyes.

"It's art."

Louise's shoulders slump no more. Her mouth, with a strand of her bob stuck in it, has hardened. She dumps her painting, her brushes, the teacher right there, and leaves the class, slamming the door. For a moment, I thought she was going to smash through the door with her belly. Everyone cracks up laughing.

I should feel victorious. I don't. That drawing isn't by me. It's the Voice: It has found another way out.

Weeks of being silent, all for nothing.

I snatch the drawing from the hands of the mesmerized teacher, and leave as well. The bell goes. I join the floods of students streaming into the corridors. I'm beside myself. I want to scream, but no, no, no, I won't, it would just be the Voice, again the Voice, screaming through me, in giant all caps.

I try to rip up the drawing, screw it up, throw it away.

It stops me from doing so.

Louise comes out of the third-floor bathrooms, wiping her chin, as if she's puked. I do an about-turn, charge down one staircase after another. It's either her or me; there can't be two Chosen Ones Here. While knowing there's no such place, I search for somewhere I can escape Its scrutiny.

As I turn a corner, a student bumps into me. He's so slight, it's he who ends up at my feet. I recognize him: the little pervert from the first floor. He doesn't apologize. Neither do I. He inspires pity more than fear, but more than anything, he disgusts me. Perhaps because he doesn't get up, doesn't want to get up. He has a groveling look, eyes that scrape the floor.

Even down there, his hands cling to the straps of a satchel he's probably had since elementary school.

I can feel the Voice rising inside me, especially for him. I don't know what It wants to say to him, and I don't want to know. I'm already far away. I take refuge in what our establishment pretentiously calls "the library."

I wanted peace. But no. A reader jumps up from her book so eagerly, then sits back down so slowly that I guess she's been waiting—no doubt for ages—for someone who isn't me.

And yet she doesn't seem disappointed.

"You're the guru from Room 1."

"I'm amazed there's still anyone who remembers that."

I've broken my vow of silence. This girl's eyes, even more than the impressive eyebrow overhanging them, disturb me. She isn't from my floor; probably from the fourth.

"Get rid of this for me, fast."

The girl examines the drawing I'm holding out to her. She screws up her eyes. Her focus becomes even sharper.

"I'm not asking you what you think of it. Just to throw it away."

My voice shakes, hoarse and furious, but for the moment, it's still mine. The girl grabs the drawing. The intensity of her concentration torments me.

"Are you going to throw it away, yes or fucking no?"

"No, thanks."

In this refusal, there's an acceptance I don't understand. The girl pulls out the chair next to hers; I collapse onto it.

"Sorry."

And yet I hadn't intended to apologize. I think back to the little pervert from the first floor I'd left on the tiles. If you're going to be a nasty piece of work, might as well own it, no? Not surprising my own grandparents fear me.

It's this girl. Behind her hairiness and politeness, I sense she's upset, but not by me. For me. And a little for herself, too, I presume.

"There are certain things one has to do on one's own," she tells me.

She closes the dictionary she was reading when I interrupted her.

"Sometimes, I turn to a random page. It's the words I don't find that most interest me."

We both look at my drawing, on the library table, between us.

I sigh.

"My teacher claims it's art. First time I've been told that. For years I've been trying my best never to go outside the lines, to draw neatly. Ten minutes of scribbling and, job done. It, this thing: it's in me, but it isn't me."

"Like a cancer?"

I agree, amazed. Exactly like a cancer.

The girl falls deep, and is lost, in thought, as if personally involved. She doesn't react to the back-to-class bell. Her thumb and forefinger pull on her bottom lip.

"It isn't you and it is you. It will always be a bit you without being entirely me. In any case, 'it,' 'you,' and 'me,' it's all a bit the same, basically, isn't it?"

I don't know if they're her words, those she's found, or will never find, either in a dictionary or anywhere else, no matter, but she's triggered something in me. Something is stirring. I cross my hands over my stomach. I have a pain. I have a pain?

"Shall I go with you to the infirmary?" asks the girl, concerned.

I'm in pain and I'm laughing.

"To the bathrooms, more likely. I know you don't know me, and I don't know you, but . . . could you help me out with a tampon?"

Iris

The study room is empty. The school is, too. Just Thingy and me, and we don't really count. It's dark through the windows, windows that don't reflect us. The neon lights flicker. We've been hanging about for hours now.

I'm coming around to the idea.

"Théophile doesn't exist."

Number Three: "I did warn you. He sees everything, but doesn't want to be seen."

Thingy jumps from one desk to another, hands in pockets. His feet produce thunderclaps in the study room, and probably well beyond, but, hey, it's not like we're in the habit of being heard.

My ass is numb from sitting too long. I pick flakes of paint off the wall beside me. The neon lights cast the chair's shadow, but not mine. I disliked the study room even when I was visible. According to Thingy, it's Théophile's fave hideout. The rare times he saw him, at any rate, were here. And never in daytime.

"He sees everything."

Number Three: "Yup."

"He sees us then."

Number Three: "Yup."

"Waiting for him."

Number Three: "Yup."

"Every evening."

Number Three: "Yup."

"What a dick."

Thingy bungles his jump between two desks. Well, if he breaks a bone, we're in trouble. The phones Here, I've tried them all. Dialing a number, no problem, but when my step-father or mother or sister answers, it cuts off every time. I've tried home eighty-three times, the police eighteen times, and the emergency services twenty-seven times. It cuts off. Every time. It's like with the mirrors, like with the neon lights: a general refusal to recognize my reality. So, there we are, if we break anything at all, we're deep in the shit.

Thingy picks up the half-cig that fell with him.

Number Three: "Might not be Théophile who's the prob-lem. Might be you. You might not be as ready as I thought."

"I managed to see your wall, you know, in the basement. I saw the future. A bit of your past, too."

Thingy crouches in front of my chair, without taking his hands out of his pockets. Like me, he's wearing clothes stolen from students, which are either too big, or too tight, and never match. We've got the same botched haircut, done with school scissors. And the same smell: the lemon soap in the bathrooms.

Number Three: "Quantum physics mean anything to you?"

"No."

Number Three: "It was our big thing, in the Top-Secret Club. The effect of the observer. Very broadly, it's because we look that everything that exists is there. Well, with Théo-phile, same thing. You have to look at him with me, and really look at him. There's no point, otherwise."

I screw up my eyes, without closing them, and I observe. The absence of my shadow on the walls. Thingy's sniffing nose. The quivering of the neon lights. The sounds of the town beyond the windows, the evening hooting, the roaming ambulances. The silence of the stars.

I lift the veil. Gauge my vision. I can see almost everything. In two dimensions, in three, in four . . . The scar on Thingy's lip is endlessly multiplied. Same with the study room. It fills up and empties, the students leave and arrive, the days go backwards. Behind Thingy's crouched figure, it's perpetual motion. His face, raised faithfully up to me, challenges me.

Number Three: "You're nearly there."

Everything freezes. It's nighttime once more, it's an empty room once more, it's us once more.

Just Thingy and me.

And Théophile.

He's standing bang in the middle of the study room, the difference being that he's got both feet planted on the ceiling. He has a seriously musty look, but more importantly, he's seriously upside-down. Thing is, he also looks seriously familiar to me. As if I'd already come across him Here, in a feet-on-the-floor version.

He smiles. A real smile, not Thingy's twisted, ironic kind. A smile that opens with a:

"Yo."

It's as if he's not really here. Even less here than Thingy and me. I must get a move on. I climb onto a desk to face him, him head down, me head up. We're like the characters on playing cards.

"Supposedly, you see everything."

"Maybe. Why?"

Very gentle, Théophile's voice. Manners soft as cotton wool. A smile like syrup. No need to ask him why he was made invisible. Can't have been a braying bullyboy.

159

"Because there's something I have to see. But I don't know how."

"Why?"

"Why what?"

"Why do you have to see it?"

"To become visible again."

"Why?"

Number Three: "Told you he was a pain in the ass."

I find him more of a pain in the neck. He might be gentle, Théophile, but there's a fierce look in his eyes. The neons cast a vibrant light around us. The desk shakes under my soles; everything's always wobbly Here. Including me. The windows don't reflect me, but they reflect Émile rather too much. Only today, he went up to the top floor of the school, although it's forbidden, and stayed there for twenty minutes, forehead against a window, watching all the others at recess.

"To prevent a little fuck from taking the plunge."

Théophile's upside-down smile broadens.

"Why for him? Why not for you?"

I'm this close to exploding, but then I look straight into Théophile's piercing eyes—I've already seen those eyes, but where? When?—and I get all his whys. If you're going to be invisible, might as well play transparency to the hilt.

"Because they're linked. Because that's what I have to see."

Théophile raises—lowers—an arm towards me. An outstretched hand. Just like that, for nothing, from one stranger to another.

"At some point, Iris, you'll have to make a choice. One can't be a spectator and an actor at the same time. I myself have chosen."

"To be a spectator?"

"No."

Théophile's hand closes on mine. He laughs.

"To be an actress."

No time to fathom his reply. I feel myself being pulled upwards, dragged out of my body and buried deep inside it at the same time. There's no more hand, no more Théophile, no more Thingy, no more study room.

There are, however, two of me. The me of now who's got her eye on the me of before. Émile's there, too. He's washing his hands in the sink. I watch my old me, who's watching Émile's back. I watch my own disgust.

I listen to our conversation.

"I'm not going to be lookout in the girls' restroom all year."

"They don't allow me . . . into the bathroom. It's only with you that I can . . . Could we eat together, in the cafeteria?"

"We can't. We're not in the same class."

"But we're still in the same schoolyard. It does count, the schoolyard. D'you remember how we'd play in our old one?"

"We're not playing in that one. We'll see."

I stare at the old me, too busy checking her image in the mirror to keep watch on the corridor. The girls are approaching; as is Émile's fate. So ugly, that me. No wonder mirrors snub me.

Here we go. The others descend. The others discover. The others decide.

"Pervert."

I don't want to be here anymore, in this restroom, but I stay. *One thing that will have to be looked at.* So, I look. I look at the old me who's looking at the girls who are looking at Émile who's looking at the old me.

"I just used the bathroom, that's all! Tell them I just used the bathroom!"

A single word would have been enough. The old me didn't say it.

"Close the door," the girls tell me.

The old me obeys, then looks away. The me of now looks. At what the girls do to Émile. I look. So open are my eyes, they dry up in their sockets. I look. I forbid myself from blinking. I look right until the end. Maybe not of the world, but it might as well be.

There. *That's* what I did to Émile.

I fall from high up; from far away; from the desk. Thingy catches me. Badly: he falls with me. A fall less hard than I'd have liked it to be. Back in the study room, in the present. Théophile has disappeared from the ceiling. The neon lights are doing my eyes in.

Thingy leans over me with all his mocking irony.

Number Three: "So. Happy?"

I turn to the wall on which all the room's shadows flicker, except Thingy's. And except mine.

I'm still Here and still not there. Invisible. I've failed.

"Leave me alone, I've got a migraine."

Pierre

Number One: "On a scale of zero to ten, zero being 'Don't agree at all' and ten being 'Totally agree,' have you observed variations in mood among your classmates and/or in yourself since the start of last term?"

"Um. Six? Then again, with all those tests . . ."

Number One: "Pretty much agree, then. Still on a scale of zero to ten, have you observed that said variations in mood occurred mainly within our establishment?"

"Um. Eight? But then, I don't see the others much after cla—"

Number One: "Pretty much really agree, then. On which day of the week are said variations in mood most noticeable?"

"Um. No?"

Number One: "You have to answer with a day of the week. Or several, it's multiple choice."

"Ah. Um. On Monday, because it's after Sunday. On Tuesday, because we have double math. On Wednesday, because it's a half-day. On Thursday, because the week's starting to drag. And on Friday, because it's before Saturday."

Number One: ". . ."

". . ."

Number One: "I don't want to influence your answer, but wouldn't there be one day more particular than another?"

"Um. Yeah. Maybe."

Number One: "Thursday?"

"Um. Yeah. Maybe Thursday."

Number One: "Thursday afternoon?"

"You don't want to influence my answer, hey?"

Number One: "Final question. On a scale of zero to ten, have you noticed, or had reported to you, any plumbing problems in the restrooms on each floor?"

"Ah, well there, zero. I'm an odd number, I don't have access to those bathrooms."

Number One: "Tough."

"You get used to it."

Number One: "Well, thanks for your contribution to our survey. It will remain anonymous and won't be used for any commercial ends."

"Um. Okay."

The student moves off with his notebook and approaches two girls, busy playing tic-tac-toe using Wite-Out on their bench. Well, whad'ya know. There was I thinking the Top-Secret Club had ceased its activities. I dig a spoon into my kiwi, get juice all over my T-shirt. The sun shines gently.

"Want some?"

I hold my spoon out to Vincent, who's sitting with me, on the tarmac, in our little corner of the schoolyard. He doesn't flinch. It's mean to taunt him like that. I think he misses food more than his family.

Five minutes to go before the bell. The kids from my class are playing with half a sponge ball. No one's paying attention to me.

Right.

I open my case, screw my oboe together, except the mouthpiece. How Vincent suddenly brightens at this!

"Don't get too excited. It's just for the fingering."

I tap away on the keys, play silent scales. The teacher has

dug up some music for beginners. If she'd given me a sheet of thingy-glyphs, it would have come to the same. Musical notation is so not my thing: I've drawn myself rows of circles to represent finger positions (a filled-in circle when I need to press a key, an empty circle otherwise) and then I learnt it all by heart. It's a bit like playing on a console, minus the race to score.

I'm definitely not at Vincent's level. When he'd play a high note, he'd wrap it in wool for you and hold it for you, his confounded note, without quavering, even wringing tears out of you. With me, it farts straight out between my fingers. But Vincent, you see, even when I let out bum notes, he nods his head. He never speaks, but he nods yes, yes, yes, always yes. He hasn't taken his instrument out of its case once since the pit. It's as if he can't. I think he misses that even more than food. But occasionally, like now, like Here, in our little corner of the schoolyard, he raises his forefinger and straightens my oboe, corrects the position of my hands, presses between my shoulder blades to unhunch me. He can't grab a spoon, but I really feel those moments of contact, sending shivers exactly where they're needed.

The bell.

I pack up my gear with, like, almost regret. When you're an odd one, you lose all impatience. And yet now, I swear, I can't wait for it to be evening; to be able, at last, to make sounds; vibrate with the instrument; breathe through it. It's not my oboe, it's my lung.

I'm clobbered by the whole class as I return to my desk at the back of the back. They lash out while still chatting among themselves. I can take it by thinking about my music.

The teacher turns up with a surprise test. The second he turns to the board to write the topic, with markers that still mark nothing, I get pelted: gravel from the schoolyard—my classmates top up at each recess. I can take that, too. I'm the odd number, the jack of spades, the lousy kid, in short, it's my thing to take the rap for the treachery of teachers.

I flinch. Got hit by a stone heavier than the rest. Blood pissing out of me. I wipe it with my T-shirt. It's my bottom lip. On the chair beside me, Vincent's not smiling at all now.

I spend the whole test in a slight state of shock. Not due to the stone; due to panic at the thought of not being able to play anymore. Vincent glares, furiously, at the twenty-four backs in front of us. I've never seen him like this. What the hell does it matter, in fact? I'm not some pro. I don't give recitals, me. At the conservatoire, they said I didn't have to audition. No one will ever listen to me. Except Vincent.

Test over, lessons over, teacher gone, I put my things away. My lip's all crusty. This evening, I'll practice my fingering, and that's it. I get the same clobbering leaving the class as I did arriving. I resist the entirely new, absurd temptation to protect my face. I sense Vincent closer to me than ever.

My case flies out of my hands. Spins up to the ceiling. Slams against the board. Lands on the dais.

General hilarity.

Right.

I don't know who did it. Not important. My forehead strikes a nose. My elbow a belly. My knee someone's balls. Vincent's lashing out with me, through me. Bodies buckle at the impact of our blows.

No one left to laugh in the classroom now. No one left to hit me, either. Silent enough to hear flies fart.

I pick up my oboe case. I leave without a word.

I'm the odd number, the jack of spades, the lousy kid, but no shit, guys, never, ever touch my oboe again.

Guy

For me, it started with the faucet. Any doofus would have twigged that white water suddenly appearing like that in the sink, well, it's not very normal and shouldn't be drunk. But me, right, I'm not any doofus, I'm the fucking *ne plus ultra* of doofuses.

I was thirsty and I drank.

I just wanted to get quickly back to class, quickly back to my seat, quickly, at the very back of the room, quickly, up against the wall, far from the others, quickly, far from the prince, quickly, very far from Sofie, quickly, get this day over once and for all, quickly, this week, quickly, this year, quickly, I thought that, anyhow, I'm fucked, quickly, just a name crossed out on the board.

I never reached the door.

Back to the bathrooms, quick, quick, quick. No need to spell out what went on in there, but it lasted, grossly, forever. I dragged myself to the infirmary, with an emergency stop at the toilets on each floor along the way. It's beyond mortifying, but when the lady came at me with her thermometer, I passed well out.

After that, a black hole. I landed back home, dunno how.

Since then, I've woken up a hundred times, gone back to sleep a hundred times.

I puke, Dad cleans up my bed, Mom cleans my body. A

proper little baby. On melba toast and stewed fruit. And then the doctor rolls up.

"It's the bowels."

Then:

"It's testosterone."

Then:

"It's all in the head."

I go back to sleep. Always the same delirious dream. I take one corridor that leads to another corridor that leads to another corridor that leads to another corridor.

I wake up. Sometimes I feel a bit better. I drag myself from my room, slump in front of the TV all afternoon, get hungry, eat straight from the fridge.

My parents say to me:

"It's good, you're less peaky. Back to school tomorrow?"

I go back to sleep. Again, those corridors lodged in my skull.

I wake up. Head-first down the can at four in the morning.

Couldn't say how many classes I've missed. I've stopped counting. What I do know is that I've just gone back to sleep, yet again, and this time the corridor in my dream finally leads to a room, the real thing, with a door and windows, if you please. And desks. And students, two by two. Apart from Sofie, sitting alone, she keeps turning around to look at my empty chair, at the back. My class. What's funny is that I see them all from the back, and the front, and the left, and the right; like, all at once.

And not only my class, in fact. All the classes on all the floors. Like, all at once.

I'm not me anymore. I'm the walls.

Each bell makes me vibrate. The sounds of sneakers, pens, insults, laughs, doors, notebooks, stairs, lessons, balls, caps, whistles, lighters, kisses, flushes, plates, trays: I'm filled with them, from the gate to the gym. With the silences, too. But especially with the rules, because c'mon, let's admit it, all that, all that's basically a game. The pairs, the prince, the odd ones, the principal: again, the game. The trends, the grades: still the game. The board, oh yes, especially that board there, nothing but names written in chalk, with the Tops always on top, the Bottoms always on the bottom: the game.

The ex-friend of the ex-guru, dragging her ginormous belly from room to room? The game. The lame oboist practicing in the parking lot with his ectoplasm? The game. The invisible ones forever rifling through pockets and trash cans? The game. The little pervert perching on ever higher windows? The game.

They all play the game. Me, I give them the setting.

And seeing as they're so keen on playing, well . . .

. . . we're going to have fun.

I wake up. Properly.

Can't remember that much of my dream, but I feel like a sock stretched out of shape by a foot that's too big. I'm me, but with contours maybe more flexible, more roomy, like I've been squatted in by something else while asleep.

Feel better. Feel clearer.

A warm breeze makes itself at home in my room, stirs the paper shade of my lamp, turns the pages of the journal I've never used, brushes, like a tomcat, against the leg poking out of both my bed and my pajama bottoms, and brings me all the smells of the building. What day is it?

The phone rings. Once, twice. No one answers it.

I get up. The apartment's empty. Parents have gone to

work. They've stuck up a conspicuous note with the numbers of a whole load of doctors. And (badly) written below: "rest well we'll be back soon."

I answer the phone, but it carries on ringing.

It's not the telephone. It's the entry phone.

"Yeah?" I say into its receiver. "What is it?"

"I've brought you the notes."

Sofie.

It's funny. I should be wondering how she knows where I live, seeing as we never hung out much beyond the gate, but I wonder nothing. I'm happy.

"Sixth floor," I tell her.

I wait for her on the landing. Yup, in my old stripy PJ's. Breath must stink. The neighbor gives me a strange look as she comes out for her run.

The elevator opens on Sofie. She's hugging a fucking ton of photocopies. In her wide-open eyes—almost hard, how she looks at me—there's a great big question she doesn't ask me.

"Come in."

I hold the apartment door open for her. The neighbor, who I'm sure lingered on purpose, looks at me even more strangely. Don't care. I'm happy.

I fill two glasses with water (bottled, of course, I avoid the faucet). One for me, to rinse my mouth. One for Sofie, to receive her properly.

She looks so carefully at our little kitchen; I discover it with her. The washing hanging between the shutters. The tablecloth with its super kitsch pattern. The tiles that don't match from one wall to the other. The sun that shines straight onto our fridge and bounces around when you open the door.

I'm happy.

Sofie sits right on the edge of my father's chair. She clings to her pile of photocopies. For the first time, I find her timid. A hairline crack, like in the glass I've just handed her.

"I've known lots of Heres," she finally blurts out. "Lots and lots."

"'Cause of your health."

Her eyebrow flies up. Doesn't often look surprised, Sofie. But my gambit surprises her, even more than me. For months I've dodged it, never daring to ask personal questions, and yet, all that time, I listened to her, to Sofie. Without my ears, I listened to her, and I heard her.

"On the first day, I was terrified. Alone. Until you spoke to me."

You're my pair. You're a Bottom. You do my homework. What a great conversation.

"I haven't been honest with you, Guy. The work I corrected for you. The advice I gave you. And when the prince made you believe he'd give his place to you . . . and after you refused, when your name was crossed out . . . I made out I still cared about you, about your future. That was hypocrisy."

When she starts fessing up, Sofie, she doesn't lower her eyes. She drills them deep into yours, sitting so straight there on her chair (well, my father's chair) and not blinking once.

"I did it for me. I wanted you to do well this year. For you to go on to high school. With me. Because before you, Guy, I'd never had . . . you're my first."

She doesn't say her first what. Doesn't need to.

I'm happy.

"I'll have to do this year again, Sofie. You'll be going to high school without me."

She nods yes. She already knew when bringing me all the lessons I've missed. Her eyelids flutter, and her lips quiver, her shoulders too, and all the photocopies she's crushing against her chest. All the hours she spent waiting for me in the library when I was moping on my chair. What an idiot I was.

"But first," I add, "I'm going to finish the year Here."

Back to the game, I think, without really knowing why.

Sofie nods again. How she's shaking! What an idiot I am.

"I told you, Sofie, I'm not like you. I might never go on to high school. I don't have any . . . (how did my father put it, again?) any direction. And it's no big deal, you know. I'll start by learning to be fine right where I am. Like now."

I don't think. I grab Sofie's hand, and so what if all the photocopies slip onto the kitchen floor.

"What you said to me and that you never should have said to me. I say it to you, too."

The Top-Secret Club

Number One: "It's going to be today."

Number Two: "You were saying that last Thursday, too."

Number One: "A simple miscalculation. The level of schmoil was still too low to produce effects in proportion to the size of the school. This morning, I took samples from all the faucets on every floor: we've reached the critical threshold. I didn't laugh, admittedly, but I did feel something."

Number Two: "It's true that I felt really weird, too, while having my piss."

Number One: "Time on your watch?"

Number Two: "2:11."

Number One: "Fine. In seventeen minutes precisely, a massive fresh arrival of schmoil will rise in all the pipes. I suggest we maintain our position in order to observe events at a distance. I've brought a pair of binoculars for you. And an exercise book to take notes."

Number Two: " . . ."

Number One: "What?"

Number Two: "Nothing. Just something that keeps bugging me. You know that valve we turned in the basement . . . I wonder if it was really such a good idea."

Number One: "An idea is never either good or bad."

Number Two: "Yeah, well, in the meantime, a massive arrival of schmoil, doesn't that risk turning everyone here a bit crazy? I mean, you keep repeating that we must find a solution to the end of the world. But isn't it we who are busy causing it, that motherfucking end of the world?"

Number One: "To find a solution to a problem, the problem first has to arise."

Number Two: "Fuck's sake."

Number One: "Science is made of paradoxes."

Number Two: "I don't know about science, but you're so stupid. Hand me the chips and the binoculars."

The Substitute Teacher

I don't like feet. My own, for starters, because they haven't changed by even a toe, despite all the nail polish I've lavished on them since the days when I was a student Here. But mainly other people's feet. The heels that drag, the soles that catch, all that fancy footwork. Feet are a whole territory. The space we allocate to ourselves, and that we don't allow ourselves. Tell me how you walk, and I'll tell you who you are. That's probably why I never use elevators or cars: to keep reaffirming myself to myself, one step after another.

Hmm. How did I get to thinking about feet?

2:13. The schoolyard is deserted at this time. An oppressive heat skulks around it. I've settled in the shade of a place tree that has survived the asphalting but is now stripped with penknives, to make the most of a break between two classes. I put away the work I was busy marking; I've lost concentration.

Why feet?

I raise my eyes. Up there, a window is open. They're there. Bare feet. Dangling at the end of two skinny legs. A kid is sitting at the edge of the void.

He's seen me. He gets up and goes in. Just like that.

Who was he? I should have looked at his face rather than his feet. Mine take me back indoors. It's even hotter inside than out. Lots of stragglers in the corridors: end-of-year slackening. Over the tacky slap of shoes, chattering and laughter.

In the staff room, there's an even more unusual cheery vibe. An impromptu gathering. Even the principal has come by for a coffee. Makes more sense, there being so few students in class.

Science Teacher: "The hardest thing is not to interfere. Sometimes, I swear, I'm itching to just headbutt all their idiotic rules."

Principal: "If they could just start by respecting the rules of this establishment, that would be, you know, something."

Literature Teacher: "That's just how it is. There are things we can't teach them. That we shouldn't teach them."

History Teacher: "It's a bit humiliating for us, but let's face facts. The learning, it's between lessons that it takes place."

Literature Teacher: "I disagree. We sow the seed. We give the keys. But beyond that, it's true, we're powerless."

Principal: "Nonsense."

I gaze at their clean, neat shoes. I think of those feet dangling in the air. *Powerless* . . .

About-turn. I charge up the stairs four steps at a time (okay, two steps.) What floor was that kid on? It's so stifling in here that all the windows have been opened, but it hasn't produced the slightest breeze. I see again, through doors that are ajar, the same false carefreeness everywhere. Bodies sprawled on chairs; rowdiness and sly smiles; vacation ahead of time. It's their feet that betray them. Stamping. Waiting for something that I, seized by an awful foreboding, guess isn't merely the next bell.

Where's the kid?

I walk back down empty-handed. After all that, I forgot my grading in the staff room.

"Yuk, yuk, gross!"

Some beaming students are splashing about in water,

right in the middle of the ground floor, somewhere between the study room and restroom. A blocked toilet? This puddle wasn't there when I went along the corridor earlier. It's huge. And white.

I walk in it, being unable to walk around it.

In the staff room, my colleagues aren't chatting anymore. They're laughing. Jerking bodies, contorted faces: they're no longer people, they're just teeth. The principal has spilt coffee on his tie. Their rocking feet horrify me.

I take refuge in the admin office, deserted by its staff. I'm shaking. Have to dial the number four times.

"You never call during the day. What's going on?"

I cling to the cable of the phone as if by doing so I might be able to hold his voice between my fingers.

"It's starting again. Like last time. At this very moment."

"Run, save yourself."

A strange way of putting it when you think about it. Is one really saving oneself by running away? On the other side of the door, which I've deadbolted, the laughter increases. Dangerously joyful. I've been immunized against that particular virus since my very own Thursday-2:28, and yet . . .

I stare at my feet, barely contained by the buckle of my pumps. I can feel the rush of blood, the urge to break free.

"I don't get myself anymore. When I accepted this position, and came back Here . . . I thought I was beyond all that."

"Thérèse."

"I was afraid they'd make the same mistakes as me, while still telling myself that they needed to, but in fact, it's me who's made them again, those mistakes."

"Please."

"The right distance. Sensible vigilance. I observe, I listen, I teach, but I don't intervene in the game anymore. What a joke! I looked down on all of them. Again."

"If you don't leave, I'll come there myself."

I smile against the receiver. Almost a kiss.

"Then you'd better get some tickets fast. Even if I'm not the one who'll put an end to the game, I'll remain with them. Until the end."

Silence on the other end of the line. The line's been cut. The door reverberates with laughter, I daren't open it.

Where's that kid?

Iris

Where's Émile?

I run from corridor to corridor, check all the windows. I woke this morning with the impression—the conviction—that the walls of our hideout were sniggering.

Yes, the walls. Sniggering, yes.

This jubilation propelled me off the gym mat that me and Thingy use as a bed. Since then, I've been running. I looked out for Émile when the gate opened, but couldn't spot him; at every bell, I infiltrate his class, the teachers record his absence hour after hour; I push open all the doors, I clamber up and hurtle down the stairs. I find him nowhere, but I know he's Here.

That it's going to be today.

It's unbearably hot. The later it gets, the worse it becomes. I pinch a plastic bottle from a student's bag. I've quit drinking from the faucets since the water turned white. Another nasty trick by the walls, that. There's a euphoric hubbub hovering everywhere that doesn't fill me with confidence.

In the tech studio, I come across Thingy. He lights one of his roll-ups with a soldering iron, as if his fingers weren't burnt enough already. He smirks so sardonically, it distorts his scar.

Number Three: "Seriously, you're still looking for him? You still haven't grasped that it's pointless? That we're pointless?"

"Move your ass and help me find him."

Number Three: "And if you do find your little buddy, what'll you do? For him, like for the others, you don't exist anymore. Just saying."

He's right. I tried to reappear and bombed big time. I looked closely at what I did to Émile, looked really carefully, but it wasn't enough. I never tried to consult Théophile again after that. Never tried anything again, period. For days now, I've been furiously gnawing my fingernails. Yesterday, I went to bed in the dark, stuck myself to Thingy despite the heat, and decided, finally, to accept it: the irreversibility of my invisibility.

But walls having a laugh first thing in the morning, no, really, that I take very badly.

Disappearance.

Murder.

Revolution.

Birth.

Then what? Is that it, the plan? Where does Émile fit into this scenario? Too lowly to appear on the bill? Or is he the star of the show?

I snatch Thingy's cig off him. I feel like filling my lungs with smoke, but that urge comes from the girls in my class. Those who, with my complicity, made Émile the handy pervert. I stub it out.

Number Three: "Oh, nice, thanks a bunch."

"One way or another, I'm getting us out of Here, me and Émile."

Number Three: "Émile, Émile, Émile! C'mon, don't waste your time. Anyhow, it's too late, the end of the world started . . . um, is it 2:46? . . . eighteen minutes ago. That's it. So might as well enjoy a quiet smoke, no?"

I edge back.

Number Three: "Watch the show with me, Iris.

I leave.

Number Three: "Watch with me, Iris!"

I'm already far away.

If Émile is thinking of swan-diving, he won't want to bungle it. I quickly go back up, yet again, to the top floor and, yet again, bump into the same lame-os clogging the stairs while laughing like crazy people. I slip on a trickle of milk. It's not milk. It's the water Here that's leaking out.

Where's Émile?

It's exasperating. I can see in two, three, four dimensions, but not what's right under my nose.

The sound of laughter makes me slow down. Trashy, that laugh. My sister's laugh. Makes sense, her classroom's also on the top floor. She's sitting ass on table, feet on chair. Screwing around with all her friends. Like the walls, she too is having fun. There's no one there to watch over them, neither teacher nor supervisor. Her mass of hair hangs down her back like some carapace, shaking every time she bursts out laughing; and does she burst out laughing, Ingrid, enough to suffocate herself. Her shorts and top barely hold her in. Her make-up's melting from the sun through the windows.

Will it be the end of the world for her, too?

I know I must get a move on, that Émile's hanging by a thread, somewhere close by. But I stay here, in this classroom, facing Ingrid. Her laugh is shrill. So shrill. What made her become so shrill? And since when? How come I've never asked myself these questions until now?

One thing that will have to be looked at.

So that's it. My own blind spot. That ended up erasing me.

I see—at last: a younger, more discreet version of my sister.

She's standing in a hospital room. With her arms behind her back, she grips her wrist hard, as if to restrain herself. On the bed in front of her, a body. And somewhere in that body, under all the tubes, Dad. Mom's not there. Too hard to count, not the breaths, the seconds between them. The old me isn't there either. Easier to play table football at the neighbors' house. I do what I didn't do at the time: I stand beside Ingrid and watch Dad die. I look at her.

She looks at me, too.

She looks at me in the present tense.

Her friends look at me, too, and they giggle even more. I'm visible again, in my scuzzy clothes, ill-matching, not my size. For the first time since my arrival Here, since Dad's death, in fact, I let myself go and I sob. My tears make them all laugh.

Almost all. A fist—loud, that fist—smashes their teeth in.

"Shut your traps, that's my sister!"

Madeleine

A drip lands on the stainless-steel sink every seven seconds; yes, I counted. I turn the old x-shaped faucet handle as far as it will go. This dripping sound, half wet, half metallic, is stopping me from concentrating on the video. I'm the only one who's bothered. Since putting the video on for us, on the lab's ancient TV, the teacher's left us "just for a minute," and hasn't been back. The others took out cigs and playing cards. In his signature barman's look, Ben's concocting cocktails in the chemistry flasks.

I always cut class when we were doing a lab. Dissections, microscopes: not for me. I couldn't stand what happened on the surface of my skin, let alone what goes on beneath it.

That was before. Now, I want to know.

On the screen, the human anatomy is broken down. I draw everything: the heart, liver, intestines, brain, vessels, innards. Control of the body regained with a pencil.

"What are you trying to prove to yourself?"

Louise's breath on my cheek. I sense it. And her smell. And the stifling heat of the lab. And the too-tight strap of my bra. And the rumblings of hunger, not even two hours after eating. And the hairs growing back, making me itch all over. Time has unfrozen inside me since that last assessment in art; no, since my encounter with the girl in the library. I can almost detect the interpenetration of an infinity of atoms—mine, Louise's, the class's, the entire world's. The girl was right, in the end, we all have in common this space full of emptiness in which everything mingles without ever touching. I was trying to escape far away from matter, but it's actually inside me, where things are scary, that my deliverance awaits.

So I scrutinize the screen, the old video, humanity sliced up, put under a magnifying glass; I scrutinize and I draw. And during this time, the Voice shuts up.

Louise doesn't:

"It's not graded, you know?"

I shrug. She persists:

"So, you're interested in meat now, are you?"

The drip-drip from the faucet has gotten faster. Not only at our bench, at all the others, too, but everyone is too busy messing around to notice. Including Louise. Ever since the teacher declared that what I'd drawn was *art*, Louise has been provoking me. It's obvious what she wants: to drag me back, with her, into our perversely familiar dynamic.

I keep my eyes glued to the screen, enough to burn my retinas, and say nothing.

"Hey, Madeleine?"

I concentrate on the documentary. I can't stop the dripping. Can't erase Louise on her stool, like one of my drawings, either. Never mind.

"Madeleine?"

Hmm. My fallopian tube's gone wrong. In the sinks, the drops are beating like metronomes set to prestissimo. The water is white.

"Madeleine!"

Louise knocks over her stool. Her shriek cuts through me like a blade. I finally look at her. The whole class looks at her. Her ginormous belly makes her back arch so much, she seems about to break. Or to give birth standing.

"You drive me insane, Madeleine, big time! For years you've been driving me insane. For years you've just opted out. Don't you understand that we're nothing without each other? Why do you think I stay Here, bored out of my brain? Because you force me to! For years I've been doing what you're totally incapable of doing! Daring to do everything you won't allow yourself to do! You have no right to change the rules like that. For it to work, you have to want to be in my place as much as I don't want to be in yours. Who do I become, hey, if you take that from me? How do I go forward if there's no one to follow me?"

The pencil drops from my hand. Around us, the others have stopped everything, the card games, the trading of joints.

They laugh.

Louise directs her rage at them.

"You, you drive me insane, too! All of you!"

But it's not going crazy that she has to worry about, it's her belly: it's disappeared. She's now floating in her still-stretched maternity dress. Not in the least pregnant, Louise. Or at least, if she miraculously was pregnant, now she miraculously isn't anymore. Back to a shapeless childhood.

How can the Voice have messed up this badly?

And still the others laugh. With a howling, hideous, hostile hilarity, while Louise pats her flat stomach in shock, and there's a pain flickering in her eyes I've never seen before.

You Are Going To Give Birth. The Voice got it wrong. Totally, terribly wrong.

"Don't make fun of me!"

Louise isn't asserting herself; she's imploring. Her arms

185

become covered in bites. No one touches her, but the laughter devours her. The more she screams, the more they laugh, and the more they laugh, the more she screams. The ridicule is killing her. The lab sinks are overflowing with water that looks like milk, the TV talks to itself, and me, I remain glued to my stool.

You Are Chosen. Entirely wrong. I chose myself, all by myself. It was, in fact, a pigeon feather. From the start, it has always been me.

Because I Am The Voice.

I stand up.

"Listen."

I didn't speak loudly. I didn't need to. The Voice, my own voice, interrupted the laughter and the screaming. A very temporary truce. Louise can barely stand, ravaged with wounds, hands on her belly, on her emptiness. The others turn all their smiles towards me, about to mock me until I bleed. Each seeking a prey so as not to be the next prey.

What a shame.

They've hurt Louise, Louise to whom everything always came too easy, Louise who wanted to taint her own perfection, Louise who embellishes the world, my own world, even—perhaps particularly—when she tries to spoil it. We have hurt her.

I'm going to hurt us in return.

I speak. I don't know what I say, I let that other voice I thought came from heaven but comes from my veins get on with it, that other me who revels in complexes. I speak. They've all forgotten that I was, for a time, their confidante. I lay out, piece by piece, their shame, everything that they try so hard to hide beneath branded clothes and clumsy make-up. I speak. They laugh at each other. I speak. I don't

186

spare myself, I lay bare my own humiliations. They laugh at me. Our skin bleeds. Their laughter subsides. I speak. They groan and suffer and bleed. I speak. They beg me to shut up. I speak. The new me—the one who was waiting to be born, the one in gestation behind the capital letters—speaks. Louise speaks to me, too. We're flayed alive. We smile at each other. We love each other.

And the fire alarm goes off.

Guy

"Alright, alright, alright. Leave your things here, line up, and calmly evacuate the building. Calmly, okay?" says the panic-stricken teacher.

It's fine, long as we can't smell smoke. I can't get over that, with all our vaping in the corridors during the year, the alarm never went off. Until today. Just my fucking luck. The moment I'm back at school, having smashed the absence record, energized and ready to pass my exams, even though I studied hard with Sofie, and so what if I fail them, seeing as, like, c'mon, there are only so many miracles . . . off the alarm goes, messing everything up. And I don't just mean the ear-splitting *nee-naw*. Outside our classroom, it's been end-of-term bedlam and hysteria for hours now. No way could I concentrate on my work, unlike Sofie who, beside me, so close to me, Sofie, has already densely filled eight pages, and is still going now, despite the alarm.

I confiscate her pen. When it's really time to go . . .

"No one leaves."

The prince has spoken. The whole class is standing, the whole class sits back down again.

The teacher protests:

"But the alarm . . . the procedures . . ."

"No one leaves," repeats the prince.

I should've known. He didn't react at all when I rolled up this morning, hands in pockets, and didn't crawl to the back of the room, didn't lower my eyes or voice, just sat at my usual place and chatted normally with Sofie. I sensed I'd shocked all present, Tops and Bottoms; I was even expecting reprisals at first recess, but then nada.

Got his own sense of timing, the prince.

The alarms are wailing, the laughter's turned hysterical outside our door, it's baking hot, fire and mayhem might be raging on every floor, but no, for him, c'mon, now's the time to sort this. He's lording it as usual on his chair. With his utility knife, he noisily cuts a very long line into the desk he's never shared with any of us.

"Outside doesn't matter."

The prince's voice is like his knife. It carves the air as if carving wood. Carves the laughter and alarms outside. Carves our silence in here.

"Even the other classes, they don't matter. The only thing that matters is me. Is you. Is here and now. In any case, there's no after for us. There are no blackboards in high school. No names. No pairs. No collection. Chaos, in other words. Over there, out there, don't kid yourselves: you're nobody."

Could've heard a pin drop. The prince turns slowly in his chair. Towards me, I'm pretty sure. I automatically looked away from his face. But I did see the knife in his fist.

"It's your lucky day, dickhead. The chance to become a Top again, regain a reputation, and remove the cross from your name on the board. To be one of us like before. Before her."

Her is Sofie. She listens without blinking, but I see the muscles of her eyelids contracting, as if she's trying to swallow the world for us with her eyes. Ah. It's because she's seen something I haven't yet seen.

That I finally do see.

Around us, at every desk, they've all unzipped their pencil cases and taken out their utility knives. The Tops, the Bottoms, the lot.

Hands are shaky. Smiles are, too.

And the teacher is, even more so.

"Please . . . in line . . . calmly."

The prince swings his arm. His knife cuts through the air and, *bang*, sticks right in our desk, Sofie's and mine. A little further, and one of us would have got it right in the face. Almost shat myself. Not a twitch from Sofie.

The prince says to me:

"You know what you have to do."

Oh, really.

At the other table, at any rate, they know. They hold the blades of their knives against their wrists. Ariane giggles behind her blade, overexcited. As for the prince, he's pulled out a second knife that's already pricking the side of his neck.

The teacher's paralyzed. Beyond the door, in all the corridors of the entire school, there's less and less laughter, more and more screaming.

What I wouldn't give for a nice, chilled Sprite . . .

I look at Sofie and she looks at me. The knife does its handstand between us. Got it—I know what the prince wants. For me to draw Sofie's blood, then my own blood, then for the whole class to draw blood, including him. A single move from me, and it'll be a bloodbath.

I pull the knife out and push in the blade.

"C'mon you guys, take it easy. Surely you're not going to do yourselves off over a blackboard."

Total shock. I've shut them all up. Serious breath-holding behind those blades.

I stand up.

"You heard the teacher. We leave our things here and go out calmly."

I make to take Sofie's hand, but she's already gone ahead. Always ahead, Sofie. And now she's facing the class. Facing the prince. She turns the force of her eyes on them. So taut, her eyebrow, it looks like it'll snap in half.

"It's true. There'll be no blackboard for you next year. No one over there will know your names. No one will tell you where your place is. You'll be little newbies, like on your first day Here."

Never speaks loudly, Sofie. You'd think the alarm would drown out her voice, but it's quite the opposite. You can hear only her.

"If you put down your knives, if you go through this door, it will still be the end of the world. Of your tiny little world. The rules you know don't exist in high school. You'll have to invent new ones. Break some. Choose your own. It's up to you."

She blows me away, Sofie. Their smiles have vanished. Blades have gone limp. There's hesitation. They might just want to live a little longer. Ariane doesn't look at all excited anymore—she's the first to drop her knife.

As for the prince, he's dropping nothing. He's standing up, too. I can only see him from the back now, but his T-shirt's drenched. He's sweating all over. His body wants blood.

Sofie's blood.

I take off, with all my weight. My yell takes off with me. I dive on the prince, who dives on Sofie. I hurl myself forward. I stretch out my arm, dislocate my shoulder, quarter my vertebrae, make myself as big as I can to grab hold of the knife in time. Shit! All those years of slouching, with all my complexes, when now, each centimeter could save Sofie . . .

Too late: blood pissing out.

Not Sofie's blood.

The teacher's blood.

"You little shit!"

No one saw him coming. Too transparent, too separate, and yet: he protected Sofie with his body. The prince stabbed him. We're all too shocked to react. All we can see is that smart white shirt as it turns redder, redder, redder . . . But hey, the teacher's still standing. He shakes his hand, covered in his own purée. In no mood for niceties now.

"What a little shit!"

Gripping the knife, the prince appears totally lost. The sight of blood, which he himself has spilt, has shaken him out of his trip. In fact, the whole class seems like it's sobered up. Knives are put away and pencil cases zipped up with expressions of fucking horror. Some even start to worry about the alarm and the screams from the corridors.

"Damned stupid little shit!"

He's so furious, the teacher, he's stopped caring about his wound. Sofie presses on it with both palms. Then the impossible occurs. A sentence that had never, in the memory of any student, been uttered by any adult to the prince:

"Your grade book, young man."

And then he keels over. Sofie holds him as best she can, tries to staunch the bleeding while keeping her sangfroid.

"Need to call an ambulance," she says.

The prince backs away. The entire class backs away with him; they all cower under their desks, pleading, as if the earth had begun to quake. Because he hasn't dropped his knife. No one dares to look at him. But I do. For the first time, blatantly, I look straight at him. And as Sofie had said, I understand why doing so is forbidden.

He's got the face of a brat. One of those brattish brats. Stuck on a teen's body, a tiny little terrified face, skin without hair or spots, a neck with no Adam's apple, a sparrow's head and puppy-dog eyes. Even the freshers on the first floor look older than him. As if the prince had never left elementary.

So that's it? What he hides behind his chains, his rings, his bling, all those trinkets from the collections: it's just that? Losing his shit so we fall for his group-suicide schtick: it's only for that? The fear of showing himself, once his reign Here is over? Meanwhile, the prince gets that I get it. He gets it and he's scared. He's at my mercy, I can humiliate him with just one word. Feed him to the class.

I sigh. I approach. I whisper:

"Sofie taught me to listen. I'll teach you to grow up. And that starts by getting out of Here and taking responsibility for your actions."

The prince's tiny little face contorts. With shame or hatred, can't be sure.

I take his knife off him, still ruddy with the teacher's blood. A teacher who's going to end up croaking in Sofie's arms, and maybe all of us with him, if we don't evacuate pronto. That's what I try to explain to the others. But a sound like I've never heard in my life drowns out my voice, the wailing in our class, and of the fire alarm, and the yelling around the school.

Music?

Pierre

I watch them. Not from the back; no longer from the back; done with backs. I watch them from the front. Twenty-four faces, furious and ravaged from all that beating . . . but laughing all the same, through what teeth they have left.

"They're crazy," I say. "They've always been crazy."

Vincent nods yes-yes. He smiles like I've never seen him smile. We're on high ground, me and him, perched on the classroom lockers, oboe cases on our knees. Skeptical spectators of the apocalypse. The day had begun pretty normally. Sun blazing, half-naked bodies. Even the teachers left us in glorious peace. Classmates talked only of the vacation, already half on holidays. There was flirting, there was showing off. There was avoidance of me.

Then all hell broke loose.

Someone brought in water bombs. For a laugh. Splats. Water weirdly white. Whole class split their sides. Not just our class, in fact—Here itself was splitting its sides; I felt it in the shuddering of the floor, the rocking of the walls. One girl spat on another girl. For a laugh. The other girl slapped a guy. For a laugh. The guy smashed a chair over some other guys. For a laugh.

Escalation.

Someone, somewhere, set off the fire alarm. Didn't help matters. Ceiling extinguishers triggered. A white rain began to fall on our floor, and with it, a stench that only I, I believe, recognized. The crazy laughter got even crazier.

In short, Vincent and I took refuge up on the lockers— particularly me, in fact, seeing as Vincent, well, he could hardly be any more dead than he is.

Not that long ago, I'd have thought all this was my fault. And maybe it is, in one way. Since I hit back, the other day, when they attacked my oboe, I've broken a pact that's much older than me; a pact made between Here and the very first odd one. But for the first time, I don't feel blame for anything. I hold myself straight.

Vincent is tapping away on his case. His fingers quicken, his eyes urge me, his smile works on me.

"You sure? I'm still a beginner."

Yes-yes. Vincent's sure. It's something more than certainty. I get the feeling it's this moment he's been waiting for since first haunting me.

"Okay, okay."

I assemble my oboe. Moisten the reed. Play.

My note's a bit shaky. I hold it, correct it, strengthen it, sustain it with all my breath, and direct it, this note, through all the frenzy and laughter. Everything slows down. Or rather, I slow down, dragging the rest of the world with me. Fists fall. The laughter dwindles, then stops. Silence seized under the siren.

They listen to me.

In two years of living together at this school, they've never spoken to me.

But they listen to me.

I slide down off the lockers without dropping either my oboe, or my note. I cross the room, between the toppled desks. The class parts to let me through; the class follows close behind me. The door is opened for me. We go out into the corridor, where tangled bodies, in ripped clothes, silently pick themselves up, ashamed and bewildered.

Everyone listens to me.

I walk downstairs, step by step. They all walk down with me.

They listen to me and they follow me.

The stairwells amplify my note and circulate it on each floor. No, it's not about acoustics. My fingers loosen. Other notes, notes I've not yet learned, follow, bursting out of my instrument. Vincent plays with me; within me. I'm imploding with music. Heads lean over banisters. Teachers reappear.

The more I blow, the more the crowds flock.

I play. Together, we get down.

I play. Together, we go into the schoolyard.

I play. Together, we pass through the gate.

I play. Together, we get out of Here.

I stop playing, but the music continues under my fingers. Vincent's playing in my place. A place I choose to leave him. I'm going to take his place at the bottom of the pit. I'm not scared, I'm happy. In my silence, I'll hear his oboe.

I'm no longer the odd number, I'm no longer the jack of spades, I'm no longer the lousy kid.

I'm no longer Pierre.

I'm Vincent.

Together (or almost)

Number Two: "Right, well . . . seems like the end of the world's over."

Number One: "Don't rush to conclusions."

Number Two: "Dunno what else you want. They're all out of danger. A bit messed up, sure, but all evacuated by that, y'know, pied piper."

Number One: ". . ."

Number Two: "What?"

Number One: "Pick up your binoculars. Look at our school. Higher up."

Number Two: ". . ."

Number One: ". . ."

Number Two: "Fuck, fuck, fuck's sake. He's going to jump, the idiot!"

I check the classrooms. One by one. I find all kinds of things—bits of broken desks and chairs, obscenities scrawled in indelible marker on boards, white puddles on the floor, streaks of blood on the walls—everything except fire.

Who set off the fire alarm? And why?

Something crunches under my heel. I've walked on a tooth. Not one of mine; they're in my pocket. Don't know how that little oboist did it, but he saved lives. My life. Almost ended up trampled to death during my feeble rescue attempt, on the first floor. Who'd have thought that pre-teens, barely out of elementary school, could flatten a sub, without leaving a crease? I won't be making my peace with feet today!

Each staircase is painful, but I still go up. Someone's worried about me out there, far from Here. I'll call you after, promise, my love, once I'm totally sure it's all over, that there's no one left to apocalypse anyone else.

Ah, in fact, yes. There are two left.

Sisters—the resemblance is striking. And talking of striking, they're not killing each other, but almost. The big one's pulling the little one's hair out; she, meanwhile, is kicking the big one's shins.

"Didn't you hear the alarm? Outside, with the others. Quickly."

"That's what I'm trying to tell her!" says the big one. "This brat refuses to leave."

The little brat would sooner pull her own hair out.

"I can't! Let me go! Émile's in Here!"

I consider the pair of them. I recognize the big one. It's Ingrid, the daughter of the mom who came to the staff room to complain. Which means that the little one . . .

I smile, with a few less teeth, but my heart's in it.

"You disappeared, you've reappeared. Congratulations."

The little one freezes and stares at me, from under the snarl of hair gripped by her sister. Her eyes bore into me like I've rarely been bored into before. The true eyes of an invisible one.

"Théophile . . . the upside-down student, that was you?"

Gosh. That's a very old and very vague memory. A distant tête-à-tête in the study room. Me above, her below. I saw her in the future, she saw me in the past. What was it I said to her again? *One can't be a spectator and an actor at the same time*. What bullshit. Of course one can.

I separate the sisters, not without a struggle.

"You say there's another student?"

"Émile. He's hiding somewhere. He's going to jump. He's waiting for right moment."

"You've already checked all the windows a hundred times!" the big one says, exasperated. "That's enough, he's nowhere. It's too dangerous here, let's get out."

I shudder. The barefooted boy of this morning: the alarm, the evacuation, that was him. My duty as an adult dictates that I first escort these girls outside, where they'll be safe.

I look at the corridor; I look at the wide-open classroom doors letting through bright sunlight; I look at the checkerboard floor tiles on which so many unfair games were played, and on which, today, like the disemboweled corpses after a battle neither lost, nor won, hastily abandoned bags are scattered; I look at that ceiling, hated no less than loved, where, in a former life, I tried my best to avoid the visible ones; I look at four years of being punished for crimes I didn't think I'd committed, of shedding my dead skins, of losing my illusions about myself, about the world, and, finally, of learning to unlearn. In short, I look at Here.

The place where one disappears, where one murders, where one revolts, and where one is born all at the same time. As long as one survives the place.

"Your sister's right. Émile must be found."

* * *

I'm lost.

The crowd's hollering so loud that I can't hear myself

199

holler. I'm jostled from all directions. I'm roasting on the spot. My T-shirt's drenched in sweat and blood—not mine, I hope. Many wounded from the fighting, a good number of broken arms. Teachers take attendance and nobody responds. The principal orders us to remain outside the gate, but above all, above all not to go back through it. Every single class out in the street. A gridlock of idiots and cars. Some hooting their horns, others shouting about terrorism, or toxic gas, or a bomb, or chemical warfare, or a nuclear attack. What's certain is that no one's laughing anymore.

One ambulance drives off with our teacher, others arrive, sirens blaring. Cops, too. The prince, dunno, think he's hiding, and I don't give a rat's ass.

I'm looking for Sofie.

She finds me. If we weren't so tightly packed already, I'd press her to me so as not to lose her again. Or rather, not to lose myself again. Because she doesn't look remotely lost, Sofie, jeez no. She charges forward and carries me with her, with such force!

She doesn't talk to me, too much of a racket.

She shows me what no one's seen except her: on top of our school, bang above the clock, right on the edge of the roof, puny as a pube, a little boy. What's he . . .

My legs catch on first. I'm running ahead of Sofie now. Some teachers and firefighters stop me at the gate. They tell me "no, no, no" by shaking their heads. Shout as I might, my voice doesn't carry. And them, they see nothing. Too high up, the little pube, too far away, too much noise, and too much sun.

Soon too late. Soon on the ground.

And with that, I lose Sofie again.

* * *

I disinfect Louise's wounds, she disinfects mine. We stole a bottle of surgical spirit from the lab just before being evacuated. I don't know what nasties you can catch when bitten from a distance, but if in doubt, double the dose.

It stings. Which I relish.

We settled on the hood of a car, in the dappled shade of a tree. Calm in the midst of chaos. Everything around us is screaming: the ambulance sirens, the school alarm, the drivers' horns, but mostly students. They want treatment, they want their parents, they want to go home.

Me, I want nothing.

I ache all over and I feel good. Louise chases away the flies with a patiently repeated flick. I have the impression of being everything: her, us, the flies, the flick, the shouts, the street and the sky. Of being Here, the vast Here, without the walls, without the tyranny of grades.

Of being.

Everyone looks glum, and it's now, far from the hilarity of school, for the first time since starting Here, maybe even for years, that I finally laugh. Everything is so funny! The adults humiliated, the adolescents ashamed, and that lanky silly boy gesticulating. Especially the lanky silly boy. I get endless pleasure watching him thrashing about despairingly and arguing at the gate no one's allowed through! It's all so clear, so obvious. I am me. I am him. I am his voice, the silly lanky lad's voice, his poor voice that's drowned out by all the other voices.

Oh yes, I am his voice and I repeat, delectably, between my lips:

"Up There. On The Roof. Help Him."

* * *

UP THERE. ON THE ROOF. HELP HIM.

I don't know where those words came from, it felt like having giant all caps in my head, but really, I don't give a shit about the how and why. Thanks to them, I'm finally searching where I need to. The tiles are scorching. And wobbly. Several went astray under the weight of the substitute teacher; a few more and she'd have plummeted. Pretty damn ironic for the old upside-down student. Whatever, she's the one who enabled me to pull myself up. My sister called her an irresponsible teacher and screamed at me to come straight down, so loud it embarrassed me, but also pleased me.

I will come down, cross my heart. With Émile.

I've gotten taller and fatter this year, despite being invisible, but it's fine, I'm still just light enough to clamber from one tile to another. They move but don't give way. I kicked off my sandals; the roof's burning my feet. I must look ridiculous and I don't care.

I reach the ridge. From here I can see everything. The town's horizon, birds in flight, the universe of the visible, and, at the other end of the roof, on the clocktower, swallowed by the sun, Émile.

I hurtle down the tiles. I'm sliding unwillingly and I use both heels to come to a halt in the gutter. Unrestricted view of the schoolyard, much too far, much too close, much too empty. The whole school is in the street, beyond the gate.

Émile hasn't budged. He's to my left, balancing on the small roof over the clock, higher than me. I can see his toes gripping the edge, as if on a pool springboard. A torrid wind ruffles his hair and shorts. So thin, Émile, not a tile shakes under him. He's almost transparent.

I shout to him:

"We're too old for hide-and-seek."

He doesn't move. His profile looks flattened against the sky. Don't even think how it would look against the ground.

"It's been 2:28 for too long."

Not in giant caps, Émile's voice. Tiny little letters. He leans forward to gaze at the stopped hands of the clock beneath his feet. Gives me such a fright. Just a gust of wind in the ass, and he'd end up right down there.

He adds, in an even tinier voice:

"We're too old for everything by now."

Something thick surges up from my stomach. It's scalding and it's bitter. It invades my mouth, then my nose, and finally my eyes. I vomit tears. Second time in one day, after holding them back for a lifetime.

"Sorry, Émile."

With butt on tiles and feet in gutter, I feel my body buckling, despite myself, as if being wrung from within.

I'm ashamed.

"Émile, stay."

He says nothing and looks down.

I lift myself up; the roof's slippery, the gutter creaks, everything's rickety, everything's pushing me towards the void, but I'm standing all the same, and I move up towards Émile.

"I'll eat your beet, you'll eat my spinach. Stay, Émile."

He looks down.

"We'll find another schoolyard where we can start everything again. Émile, stay."

He looks down.

"I'll never let anyone stop you from pissing again. So, stay a bit longer. Stay with me."

He looks down. I stretch out my arm. My hand beckons his.

"Stay."

* * *

Number One: "Right. Let's put the binoculars away. This time it really is over."

Number Two: "Seems like it, yeah."

Number One: "You crying?"

Number Two: "It's Number Three. I miss him, fuck's sake."

Number One: " . . ."

Number Two: " . . ."

Number One: "The whole experiment was worthwhile. We've gathered lots of data. We'll find a solution to the next end of the world. And if not to the next one, to the one after that."

Number Two: "Okay."

Number One: " . . ."

Number Two: " . . ."

Number One: "Number Two."

Number Two: "What?"

Number One: "Thanks."

Number Three: "I miss you, too. Assholes."

New School Year

You

Today, you decided that things wouldn't be like yesterday. Yesterday doesn't really count. It was the first day, after all. You only had a single class, and even then, it was to give all of you the rules, the timetable, and a plan of the school.

It doesn't count.

You arriving twenty minutes late doesn't count. Forgetting your school bag in the car doesn't count. You landed yourself with the worst desk in the classroom, right opposite the teacher, in the very front row, with a boy who smells really-really bad beside you and a load of sniggering behind you, but that, too, doesn't count.

It's today that everything starts properly.

Here you are in the schoolyard, nice and early. For now, you don't have any friends to talk to. It's drizzling. Groups have already formed under the shelter, your old classmates from elementary school are scattered here and there. Apart from you, only one student is on the sidelines, and since it's the boy who smells really-really bad, you don't approach him, either. You feel alone, but make sure not to show it. You retie your shoelaces, one after the other, as slowly as possible. You pretend to check something inside your bag. You take the chance to reread your timetable. You walk in the rain, hands in pockets, with false nonchalance.

Is it always this long before the first bell?

You look right up high, above the four floors of the school, at the face of the clock. It's mercilessly accurate.

Two other students are gazing up there, too.

"That's where he jumped from."

"I tell you he didn't jump."

"Yes, he did jump."

"No, he didn't jump."

"So you've seen him Here, yourself, since then? He jumped."

"He changed school, dipshit. He didn't jump."

"I know a guy who knows a guy who saw him jump."

"He didn't . . . oh, fuck's sake, what the hell do we care anyway? We don't even know the dude's name anymore."

The two students move off, and you, you wonder who they might have been talking about. You notice that there was a third student with them who hasn't moved. A *big one*. He stands very straight in the rain, his overlong bangs sticking to his nose. As well as his backpack, he's carrying a strange case in one hand.

He's staring at the clock:

"It'll stop again. One day or another."

You don't know if he said that to you, or to himself. You're intimidated, but you still ask:

"The dude. Did he jump or not?"

The *big one* smiles at you. You've never seen a smile like it. Reminds you of an elastic band.

"Well, that depends on you."

The bell rings. The *big one* is far away now. You didn't understand a word of it.

You go up to your classroom on the first floor. With each step, you wonder whether the dude jumped or not. You don't know why, but it's become extremely important to you. No, really, today things mustn't be like yesterday. You must quickly change desk, find yourself a better seat.

Preferably not too close to the boy who smells really-really bad. You stop before going in to join your classmates. Something's different. Something disturbing.

A blackboard. Right in the middle of the corridor. And on the blackboard, names have been written in chalk. All the names of your class. Your name, too. You look more closely. The names go two by two: one name on top, a line, one name on the bottom.

Your name is beneath the name of the boy who smells so bad. What does it signify and why does it scare you this much?

"I was sure I'd find you here."

You jump. A *big one* even *bigger* than the student holding that case—than all the *big ones* in the whole school, in fact—is leaning over you. It's not to you that he spoke, but to the board. And yet, you think, his name isn't on it. He takes some chalk and draws lines everywhere. When he's finished, he puts the chalk down, slaps his hands to remove the dust, and then is off again. Just like that.

On the board, it's no longer single lines between the names. Between your name and the name of the boy who smells really-really bad. It's "equals" signs.

Suddenly, you're not scared anymore. Because yes, it's up to you.

You hear yourself declaring in a new voice:

"He Didn't Jump."

And you head into class.

About the Author

Christelle Dabos was born on the Côte d'Azur in 1980 and grew up in a home filled with classical music and historical games. She now lives in Belgium. *A Winter's Promise*, her debut novel, won the Gallimard Jeunesse-RTL-Télérama First Novel Competition in France, and was named a Best Book of the Year by critics and publications in the US, including *Entertainment Weekly*, *Bustle*, *Publishers Weekly*, and *Chicago Review of Books*. *A Winter's Promise* was named the #1 Sci-Fi/Fantasy title of the year by the editors of the *Amazon Book Review*.

The Mirror Visitor

Book 1
A Winter's Promise

Ophelia possesses two special gifts: a talent for seeing into an object's past and the ability to travel through mirrors. Her peaceful existence on Anima is interrupted when she is promised in marriage to the taciturn Thorn, a member of a powerful clan from a cold and distant ark. A pawn in a dangerous game that will have far-reaching consequences for her entire world, Ophelia must navigate the lies and machinations of her fiancé's clan in order to survive in this first installment of the internationally best-selling Mirror Visitor series.

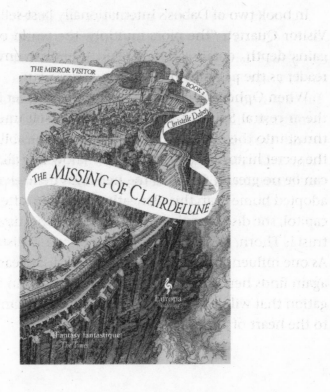

Book 2
The Missing of Clairedelune

In book two of Dabos's internationally best-selling Mirror Visitor Quartet, "the plots multiply, the world of the Arks gains depth, details abound, and the story envelops the reader as the pages fly by." (*Le Monde des ados*)

When Ophelia is promoted to Vice-storyteller by Farouk, the ancestral Spirit of Pole, she finds herself unexpectedly thrust into the public spotlight. Her gift—the ability to read the secret history of objects—is now known by all, and there can be no greater threat to the nefarious denizens of her icy adopted home than this. Beneath the golden rafters of Pole's capitol, she discovers that the only person she may be able to trust is Thorn, her enigmatic and emotionally distant fiancé. As one influential courtier after another disappears, Ophelia again finds herself unintentionally implicated in an investigation that will lead her to see beyond Pole's many illusions to the heart of a formidable truth.

Book 3
The Memory of Babel

In the gripping third book of Christelle Dabos's best-selling saga, Ophelia, our mirror-traveling heroine, finds herself in the magical city of Babel, guarding a secret that may provide a key to both the past and the future. After two years and seven months biding her time on Anima, her home ark, it is finally time to act, to put what Ophelia has discovered in the Book of Farouk to good use. Under an assumed identity, she travels to Babel, a cosmopolitan and thoroughly modern ark that is the jewel of the universe, and where automata have taken over the humblest jobs from humans. But under the surface of this seemingly peaceful and orderly ark social unrest stirs, fed by the memories of a fateful ancient purge and the inhabitants' growing fear of being replaced altogether. Will Ophelia's talent as a reader be enough to prevent her being lured into a deadly trap by her ever more fearful adversaries? Will she ever see Thorn, her betrothed, again?

THE MIRROR VISITOR

BOOK 4

Christelle Dabos

THE STORM OF ECHOES

It's Pullman in a beret and Breton
stripes... We're on the edge of our seats.
The Spinoff

The Storm of Echoes offers a chilling but
simultaneously euphonic experience.
Priscila Ball, *The Daily Californian*

Europa
editions

Book 4
The Storm of Echoes

In this gripping finale to Christelle Dabos's internationally best-selling fantasy saga, the mirror-traveling heroine Ophelia and her husband Thorn discover that the truth they have been seeking has always been hidden behind the mirror.

Ophelia and Thorn are at the center of a great, universal game in which the stakes are life and death. Their arrival at the Deviations Observatory, an institute shrouded in secrecy and overseen by a sect of mystical scientists, signals hope. The destruction that has consumed their world may soon come to an end, bringing about a return to harmonious coexistence. Everything hangs in the balance, but there is one great mystery remaining, and reaching its source is harder than either Ophelia or Thorn could have imagined.